C000110450

WORDS AND WOMEN:
THREE

2016

CAMEO

First published in 2016
By Unthank Books
www.unthankbooks.com

Printed in England by

All Rights Reserved

A CIP record for this book is available from the British Library

Any resemblance to persons fictional or real who are living, dead or
undead is purely coincidental.

ISBN: 978-1-910061-34-3

Edited by Lynne Bryan and Belona Greenwood

Cover design by Rachael Carver

Strictly Belly Dance © Susan K Burton 2016; *Boy With Gun* © Caroline
Davison 2016; *The Accomplice* © Sara Keene 2016; *The End Of The Line*
© Glenys Newton 2016; *Scalpelling Through* © Sarah Evans 2016; *Room
Service* © Claudine Toutoungi 2016; *Calentitos* © Deborah Arnander 2016;
Still Life © Danusia Iwaszko 2016; *The Second First Time* © Dani Redd
2016; *Looking For Jim Morrison* © Victoria Hattersley 2016; *Atacama* ©
Ann Abineri 2016; *Sacraments* © C.G. Menon 2016; *Folding* © Patricia
Mullin 2016; *Leda's Swan* © Margaret Meyer 2016; *Colin* © Julie Kemmy
2016; *I'm Not Christiane* © Nicola Miller 2016; *The Colours Of Snow* ©
Louise Tree 2016; *The Friends* © Kathy Mansfield 2016; *Charis* © Sharon
Eckman 2016; *Thin Walls* © Sarah Ridgard 2016; *A Canary In Kabul* ©
Antoinette Moses 2016; *You're In The Movies, Huni* © Isabelle King 2016.

CONTENTS
WORDS AND WOMEN: THREE

Editors' Note – Lynne Bryan & Belona Greenwood, 7

Preface – Emma Healey, 11

Strictly Belly Dance – (creative non-fiction) – Susan K Burton, 17

Boy With Gun – (fiction) – Caroline Davison, 27

The Accomplice – (fiction) – Sara Keene, 35

The End Of The Line – (non-fiction) – Glenys Newton, 45

Scalpelling Through – (fiction) – Sarah Evans, 53

Room Service – (fiction) – Claudine Toutoungi, 63

Calentitos – (fiction) – Deborah Arnander, 69

Still Life – (fiction) – Danusia Iwaszko, 79

The Second First Time – (fiction) – Dani Redd, 89

Looking For Jim Morrison – (fiction) – Victoria Hattersley, 99

Atacama – (fiction) – Ann Abineri, 109

Sacraments – (fiction) – C.G. Menon, 115

Folding – (fiction) – Patricia Mullin, 125

Leda's Swan – (fiction) – Margaret Meyer, 135

Colin – (fiction) – Julie Kemmy, 145

I'm Not Christiane – (fiction) – Nicola Miller, 155

The Colours Of Snow – (fiction) – Louise Tree, 165

The Friends – (fiction) – Kathy Mansfield, 173

Charis – (fiction) – Sharon Eckman, 183

Thin Walls – (fiction) – Sarah Ridgard, 193

A Canary In Kabul – (memoir) – Antoinette Moses, 203

You're In The Movies, Huni – (fiction) – Isabelle King, 213

Editors' Note

– Lynne Bryan & Belona Greenwood –

Words And Women started out almost by accident five years ago with an ad hoc assembly of women writers and musicians to celebrate International Women's Day. Since then, we have showcased and celebrated women writers who live in the East of England, at all stages of their professional careers. We work in the community encouraging girls and women of all ages to find their voice. We have hosted vibrant and eclectic reading events, reached out to women musicians and singer songwriters, commissioned large-scale site-specific art, held exhibitions of contemporary drawing and done all in our power to commission new writing. *About*, funded by Arts Council East, gave four women writers the opportunity to produce new work for page and performance, the texts performed by a quartet of actors. Winners of Words And Women's annual prose competition have gone on to receive agent representation.

It would be easy to think we are not needed. Why should we make a fuss about providing women with more public space when there are plenty of high profile women writers out there? But as long as female authors feel it is necessary to disguise their gender on the cover of their books, using initials or adopting a male pseudonym in order to be read by men and boys, we will be around. And while there is an imbalance in the number of female to male books reviewed in the literary press, we will do our best to bring brilliant women's writing to public attention.

Our annual competition is an opportunity for us to bring to readers a range of voices, a slew of themes, and a stack of story-worlds. It's exciting to find the new and most original and poignant tales and to print them. We hope you enjoy these very human, very female words.

Preface

– Emma Healey –

Can I be honest? I was dreading the judging process for the Words And Women prose competition. When the manuscripts were delivered to me in December I was excited to open the package and see what was in there, but also very reluctant to begin reading.

This is because judging a short story competition is not like normal reading. Usually I choose what to read, how long for, whether to continue and when to stop. It's a personal thing and part of the experience is the initial decision to pick up a particular book or turn to a certain article, to see the cover or short description and say: yes I want to know more. But for this anthology I *had* to read the forty longlisted pieces in the envelope of manuscripts, and had to read them properly, in their entirety and with due concentration.

I don't usually read with a set of rules. I might analyse as I go, but it's with a hazy goal, to understand a structure or notice a device or find some inspiration buried in the story. I'm not usually deciding anything as concrete as who should be included in an anthology. But I wanted to be as fair as I could, so although I would normally let myself devour as many pages as I wanted, in this instance I determined I wouldn't read more than four stories in a day, because I might not do justice to the last piece at the end of a long reading session. I also decided I would never read any of them early in the morning or late at night, because I might be too tired to appreciate nuance or subtlety, and that I wouldn't listen to music or sit with them in a café, because the rhythm or atmosphere might unfairly influence my understanding or enjoyment of the work.

I was taking my role seriously. And this seriousness added to my apprehension. What a relief then to find that so many of the stories and essays I'd been sent were engaging, coherent and emotionally honest, full of keen observation and vivid images.

One of the most important questions a writer can ask herself is: Why should a reader read *my* story, or essay or novel? Why should they give up their time, their TV watching schedule, their smart phone games or internet browsing for me, for something I've created? And it seems that all the writers of the works in this anthology *have* asked those questions of themselves. In *Folding* by Patricia Mullin, a story which starts with mysterious packages, intrigue is used to draw the reader in, whereas Susan K Burton, the author of *Strictly Belly Dance*, gives us a new perspective on Japan with sparkling humour. Not only are the stories all the more engaging for this, but I felt closer to the writers too.

Which leads me to the next way in which competition judging is so different from my everyday reading experience: I usually know who the author of anything I read is. Even if I don't immediately recognise the name I can always Google them to find out more about their other works, their background and interests. In contrast this process was entirely anonymous, I had no clues to the identity or intention of the author other than the text itself. Which is as it should be, perhaps, but it's still strange in this age when publishers promote the personality of an author as much as the quality of her words.

Had the writer of *The End of the Line*, a detailed and moving account of 'The Jungle' refugee camp at Calais, actually been there? Was she an activist, trying to highlight the struggles facing the inhabitants of this infamous place? Should that matter? And if that didn't matter, what did?

In order to answer this question I came up with a checklist, a way of assessing the pieces in the most logical way. I gave points for interesting handling, clever structure, clarity, dialogue, and imagery. Reading and rereading, assessing and reassessing. I also looked for sympathy— pieces which made me believe in and feel for the characters—and resonance. This was something I could only gauge after I'd put the manuscript down, but finding myself haunted by a piece of writing is a good sign of its reach, and I have found myself thinking about many of the entries over the past few weeks, unable or unwilling to let them go. I also looked for humour, finding it in a great deal of the writing, but used to brilliant and poignant effect in Claudine Toutoungi's *Room Service*, a darkly playful story about a hotel cleaner. The last element I looked for was topicality—work that explored current events and controversial issues, and this, as well as every other point on the checklist, was evident in *Scalpelling Through* by Sarah Evans. Taking on the thorny issue of gender identity, it is a funny, brave, provocative and well-handled story and a very worthy winner. I hope readers of this anthology will agree, whether they are using my pedantic checklist or not!

Strictly Belly Dance

– Susan K Burton –

La Habana was a salsa club and 'dance academy' above a fried chicken restaurant in the business district of Nagoya, central Japan. Flyers taped to the walls up the narrow staircase showed swarthy Latino men in open-necked shirts with their arms wrapped tightly around the waists of tiny, over-excited Japanese women. Tuesday was the club's quiet night and although the bar was open, no-one ventured onto the wooden dance floor with its wall of mirrors and set of bongos in the corner. So on Tuesdays they held belly dancing classes instead.

I took up belly dancing to make friends and improve my Japanese. My workplace, the language faculty of a local university, was largely male and English-speaking. Becoming an *okusan* (a housewife, literally a 'Mrs Interior') was considered to be a woman's *eikyu-shushoku*, her 'eternal employment', and a former prime minister once declared that women who 'don't even given birth once' should be denied a state pension since it is 'supposed to take care of and reward those women who have lots of children.' Consequently, Nagoyan women over the age of 25 tended to disappear from the city's streets when school let out, only making a reappearance the following morning when they could be seen hanging their family's futons to air on apartment balconies. Finding Japanese female friends who were up for a bottle of hot saké, a discussion on equal pay and a karaoke singalong was like hunting an Amabie, a Japanese ghost mermaid. Belly-dancing might seem an odd choice but it was obviously going to be a women-only class, and a

19

poster on the staircase said that the teacher was New York-trained and spoke some English.

I persuaded my British friend, Avril, to join me because she had something I lacked - natural rhythm. We climbed the stairs, paid our 2,500 Yen and waited. Just before seven o'clock, around a dozen women hurried in, obviously having rushed straight from offices where their uniforms - straight skirt and waistcoat combinations in scratch-resistant black or beige polyester, white shirts and flat shoes - marked them out as OL's (Office Ladies), shop staff and bank clerks. They took turns stepping behind a screen to change.

To jazz up our sweatpants, Avril and I had rush-ordered hip scarves from Tokyo. The Japanese women had apparently bought the rest of the shop: chiffon skirts in sherbet pinks and mint greens, sequined bras, beaded halter tops, sparkling necklaces, bracelets, anklets, dangling earrings, and flower hair decorations. And they coordinated. For an hour's lesson, they dressed for a Saturday night at the sultan's palace.

We mustered on the wooden dance floor facing the wall of mirrors and began our warm-up dance. Mari, our teacher had long black hair 'like a raven in the rain' as the Japanese say. She wasn't fazed by foreign faces and while she did speak English, since we were copying her movements we didn't need to speak at all. We just needed to lift and drop to the beat of the darbuka drum, sway and slide to the eerie rasp of the ney flute, and twist and turn to the aud lute. The music seemed to transport us a vast distance, far from Japan and the long working day. I wondered where the music was taking the office ladies, and whether they practised their figure eights by the photocopier when no-one was looking.

One hour later, we claimed our free Oolong tea and sat at the bar watching the advanced group warm up. During the class, no-one had spoken to us but, having spent a year studying English in Canada, Ritsuko, in a pair of flared trousers that had followed her over from a salsa class, didn't hesitate to mambo over, post-class cigarette clamped between her lips, and introduce herself.

Ritsuko was a special needs therapist who had co-founded a day care centre for kids with mental and physical disabilities. Occasionally she came late to class because a parent had neglected to pick up their child. Once she phoned to say she was still at the hospital with a girl who had appeared at the centre with burns from a hair straightener, inflicted by her mother.

Ritsuko's friend, Michiko, was a despatch worker, a temp, and said she knew Toyota was in financial trouble when they stopped replacing the soap in the toilets. Michiko was engaged to a married salaryman who had just left his wife and their autistic child. Ritsuko disapproved and said so, but they remained close friends. Michiko said that because of the risks, she had given up any thoughts of a baby of her own.

With a glossy, page-boy haircut and exaggerated mannerisms, Shinobu was a playful dancer who let loose a deep, throaty laugh whenever she got a move wrong. She wasn't a regular but was always fun company when she did appear. Every six months, our group would perform a dance at a public venue and for a month beforehand much of the class would be devoted to perfecting the routine. Avril and I always opted out. As foreigners, we got stared at enough in public without removing half our clothes. Shinobu also declined to join, citing compulsory overtime. We'd sit at the bar and chat. Shinobu had work problems but any attempt to question her about them simply elicited the response, 'Saaa ...,' a sort of Japanese sigh which implies that things are too troublesome even to put into words. Some evenings she'd just spend the hour nursing an Asahi Super Dry and saying she didn't feel much like dancing. Then she didn't feel much like talking either. Soon after, she stopped turning up at all.

One evening, Ritsuko pointed out that the same woman stood next to me every week. She arrived earlier than the others, never spoke to anyone and, after changing, swept straight onto the dance floor to warm up in front of the mirrors. As she bumped and body waved, she would watch herself in wonder, her mouth forming a perfect 'O'. 'She's obviously enjoying herself,' observed Ritsuko wryly, and named her 'Miss Ecstasy'. Miss Ecstasy wore her hip scarves long, gipsy style, the fringing dusting the floor as she dipped and circled. She continued to admire herself until the rest of the class shuffled into position for the warm-up and then, as we all jostled for dancing room, she'd manoeuvre tactically into a space right next to me. 'Maybe she wants to copy what I do,' I suggested.

'Maybe,' mused Ritsuko, which is polite Japanese for, 'Are you kidding me?' 'Or perhaps next to you she just looks so much better.' I noticed she kept well away from Avril.

None of us dared invade the orbit of Ningyo-chan, the Little Doll. The Doll was well under five foot, so tiny she could shop at Gap Kids, but with a figure like an animé cartoon cutie: a voluptuous bosom, rounded hips and a waist you could fit a pinky ring on. Her movements were minute and precise. The expression on her face never changed. While some of us looked as if we were giving birth mid-routine, the Doll always looked serene.

Through my dancing classmates I gained access to Japanese culture in a way that had been closed off to me before. They taught me what brand of soy sauce to buy, where to get the car blessed, and how to get discount vouchers off the internet for the Big Echo karaoke bar. When Japan's glossy magazines urged us to eat collagen-rich foods for good skin and 'nice body', we went out to eat chicken on bamboo sticks. I gamely chewed through skewers of thumb-sized livers, tiny jewel-like hearts, small intestines, and gizzards, but at *nankotsu* (cartilage and connective tissue formed into a lollipop shape) I reached my culinary limit. To girly giggles and Ritsuko's guffaws, I wretched as globs of fat-soaked gristle popped and crackled in my mouth. 'Very healthy,' Michiko assured me. 'Lots of collagen.'

Like many of the women, Michiko was flat chested. She solved this by filling her bra with plastic 'chicken fillets' and debuted them at the restaurant. 'They feel so real!' she assured us and proved this by grabbing one of my breasts and one of hers and squeezing. Japanese people tend to be undemonstrative. They bow instead of shaking hands, while hugging and cheek-kissing are endured with stoic embarrassment. But when you're one of the girls, Japanese women are extremely tactile, the division between where you end and they begin largely dispersed. I was now one of the girls. Unfortunately for Michiko, her chicken fillets weren't as real as she'd hoped. As soon as she shimmied onto the dance floor, they fell out. 'You'd better eat more collagen,' I suggested.

One evening, Mari invited a guest teacher, Ranya, her classmate from New York. While Mari's speciality was glides and turns, Ranya was a well-built American who could carry off the raunchier moves. 'Think of your bosom as a shelf,' she encouraged the class, 'and imagine you have drapes hanging from it. Make a boob curtain.' I could make a boob curtain. So could Ritsuko and the Doll. Avril could have sheltered the entire class from the rain under hers. Poor Michiko.

During exam season, with papers to grade, our attendance was patchy. One evening, Mari said to Avril and me, 'If you don't attend regularly you won't improve.' 'But we're not here to improve,' we responded. 'We're here to have fun.' I'm not saying we didn't try our utmost to get the moves right. We bought the CD's and practised our 'Bambi Saidi' routine at each other's apartments on weekends. But our approach to the classes differed from that of our classmates. We expressed, as the Japanese say, a 'wrong attitude'. We laughed, we fooled around and there was the time I had to be physically removed from the bongos. Other than Ritsuko, the Japanese women remained straight-faced, serious in their pursuit of perfection. They soon moved up to the advanced group. Then after a while, they stopped coming.

The last time we went out for chicken was before I moved up to Tokyo. The women ordered *bonjiri* and, not wanting to be caught out, I asked the waitress in Japanese what that was. Stumped for a mime she hurried away to the kitchen area where I could see an animated discussion taking place with the manager and chefs. Someone got out a smart phone and began tapping. I was halfway through my second skewer when the waitress leaned close to my ear and whispered in English, 'Chicken arseholes.'

A year later, I met up with Ritsuko at the Casablanca, Nagoya's only Moroccan restaurant, a small, cave-like venue festooned with dusky red drapes and lanterns which swung in the breeze whenever a customer opened the door. As we shared spicy harissa soup and steaming briwats, a voice from the back of the cave announced the start of the evening show and, twisting and twirling from the kitchen came Mari in her signature scarlet costume. She was joined by her regular partner Sana in ice blue, and together they performed a dance with long curved swords which they clashed together in time to the music. It was a deft performance in a room no wider than a bus.

Towards the end of the show, Mari and Sana began pulling diners to their feet to dance with them. Most wiggled with embarrassment then sat back down as soon as they could slip away. Others began furiously checking their phones and refusing to make eye contact. But a few women did leap up with enthusiasm to whirl and weave their arms above their heads. 'Look!' squealed Ritsuko, grabbing my arm. 'It's Miss Ecstasy.' And there she was, gyrating ecstatically in front of the diners, heavily pregnant.

Michiko married her salaryman. She still temps. Avril married a welder, had two kids and teaches at a local university. The Doll, whose name turned out to be Hatsune, dances at the Casablanca on Friday nights and teaches at Mari's new Ya Salam belly dance studio. After two years without a holiday, Ritsuko quit her job at the day care centre and went back to Canada. In Tokyo, I opted for yoga classes instead, another hobby in which I was out-dressed by the rest of the class. I don't know whether my Japanese improved at La Habana but it was through my classmates that I discovered the reality behind the Mrs Interior façade, and learned that there were women out there who, albeit within Japan's patriarchal confines, were going out and enjoying themselves, making real life choices, and eating way too much chicken. I couldn't connect with these women in their culture, and our paths didn't cross in mine. It was a third culture, belly dancing, in which we were all strangers that brought us together for a short time in a tiny bar above a fried chicken shop.

'Did you ever find out what happened to Shinobu?' I asked Ritsuko as we sipped mint tea, post-show. Ritsuko shook her head. 'He probably became too busy. You know he was an important company director, don't you?'

Boy With Gun

– Caroline Davison –

He'd taken his gun and he meant to do it. Yes, he would do it this time and then it would all be over.

A March wind was blowing up on the tops, clouds flying. It pleased him, the wind blustering that way, forcing the stunted trees to scrape and bow in the face of his rage.

Mother came to the kitchen door just as he was leaving.

'Will you be long?'

There was flour on her apron. Baking. He knew why. But even she couldn't reach him now, with that look in her eye, same as she used on father. It riled him, to think she could use that same look. He hadn't ever done her harm. Why would she look at him that way?

'I thought I'd bag a rabbit.'

'You'll be back for tea?'

'Yes,' he said, though it was a lie.

In the porch he paused to light a cigarette, inhaled deeply, before turning up the track towards the smooth green haunches of the downs. He'd taken that path a thousand times. But today was to be the last and so each hedge, or gate, each patch of rough grass was suddenly beloved. All the colours were flooding in.

He saw how the hill wasn't flat green, like he'd painted it as a child. In the deep shade it was blushed purple, like a pigeon's breast, and where the sun skimmed the top it shone white. The tree bark, rumpled grey, reminded him of the stuffed elephant leg he'd seen for sale once at the village fete, thrown out from the big house. His hands went up to cover his ears against the shrill din of a blackbird, it cut through his brain so, like a thin wire.

Memories bubbled up. How he used to play in the autumn puddles there with his sister, stamping and splashing, Joan screaming with laughter. They'd make boats out of leaves and throw stones at them, watch them capsize. Pick flowers for their mother, or blackberries. Once they'd found a kitten. The little scrap was sickly and they'd taken it back to the cottage, fed it milk. It was gone by the morning and mother said it had probably trotted off home. Later he realised father had drowned the creature. They had no spare for useless pets.

When things were bad, they'd run right to the top, him holding Joan's hand, pulling her along, to get away from father in one of his rages. Up on the ridge they were safe, looking down on everything, the cottage like a toy. It was hard to imagine father thumping mother when you were up there, so high. Things were too small to do any harm. He and Joan would play for hours, roll down the slopes, make themselves dizzy, chase around with their arms flung out, pretending to be aeroplanes.

He paused, dropped his fag end and pressed it into the chalky mud with his boot. Who would have thought Joan would get killed by a real metal aeroplane sweeping over their hill to bomb Lewes? Funny to think of that. One minute she was buying bread for their tea, the next she was dead, the baker's shop on top of her. Maybe the pilot forgot it was real people going about their business down there, everything so small.

The noise of the aeroplanes, and the bombing had set his father trembling and gibbering in the corner like a lunatic, his arms over his head. It was shameful, the way he cowered and snivelled just at the noise of planes. Mother said the last war had hollowed him out, that he'd never been the same since. She barely stopped crying, what with the planes and the bombs and Joan dying. He'd been sad about his sister, she'd been a good girl. But when he thought about that kitten drowned, a tear came to his eye.

So here he was, on his way to the top of the downs thinking about ending the gnawing in his stomach, and maybe it was because he was half way to thinking himself dead that he started seeing all the colours and hearing the birds and the wind raging. Each thought that came into his head was a dewdrop hanging on the end of a twig, ripe, glittering in the sun, ready to burst. He knew that he would be hollowed out by the war, just the same as his father, and that it had to end.

He was a good way up the track now, sweating with the effort of the steep climb. Looking down towards the water meadows he saw the familiar silver curve of the river at the foot of the hill. He stopped and shifted the gun where it was rubbing, his hand running over its familiar smooth wood, the cool of the barrel. And it was a jolt, like it had gone off, to think that this old friend would soon finish everything, the view across the valley, the wind, the mud of the track, and the smooth rump of the hill rising up above him.

Susan slipped into his thoughts then. She would cry when she heard. He felt some satisfaction at the idea. That would teach her to mess with those Canadian boys, and give him the cold shoulder. She would think it was her fault. He minded that he wouldn't know what love was, how it might have felt to lie with her, what glory there might have been in her skin against his. But she was a thin mist that evaporated in the heat of his real fury.

He had dreamt about how he would change his life when he was

31

a man. How he would pin his father against the wall and shake him till his teeth fell out. How he would take proper care of his mother, make her smile. But the coming of age had turned into a curse not a blessing. The days would not stop, they kept rolling over, one after the other, faster and faster, an avalanche of days. As he trudged up the hill, the last ounce of his childhood spilled from his pocket, scattered behind him. He would be conscripted. Already, he was hollow. His own children would cower, his wife flinch.

So, better to finish it before it started. That's what he was thinking. There was a dip, just along the ridge, something like a green bowl, in which he and his sister used to shelter, below the wind that always raked across the edge. There was stillness there. He imagined himself lying down on the soft wet earth, letting the bad blood run out of him.

At the top he turned to the view across the river valley, searing the image onto the back of his eye as if the memory might linger after his death, a ghost of muted greens. In the far distance below, down by the bridge, he saw a figure. He could make out the long brown coat and skirt of a woman. Something made him stop, seeing her gaze down at the shining water. For a moment they both watched the space between the living and the dead.

She was balanced on the edge of the bank. He thought of the figure-head of a ship, leaning out, face turned to the sea. A sudden movement, the flinging away of a stick, and she sank into the river. There was a beauty in it, the way she let herself fall, a surrendering through the cool flat surface of life into the underworld. As he gazed on, the woman in the distance quietly absented herself. The blackness of her skirt billowed up briefly but she was submerged, and soon the woollen folds wrinkled, shrivelled, disappeared. The skin of the river returned to a mirror. He imagined her sliding like a sleek brown fish below, out into the sea's abyss.

He didn't raise the alarm. What would be the point? She was too far away. Already the fast flowing tide was speeding her on the journey. Neither did he think to pray for her soul, but his mind travelled with her, a sympathetic companion through the dark currents. While life petered out so effortlessly before him a soft calmness settled, as though the woman had taken his cares, and slid them into her pockets. She might have said, 'Look, boy. This is a proper leave-taking of the world, a calm relinquishing. You stay.' He felt foolish and clumsy, with his gun and dreams of shooting his brains out, before he had even lived.

The raw wind cut under his coat unnoticed as he stood on the hill for hours, watching. A man ran out to the river bank, found the stick, hurried away. Other men arrived, walked up and down the bank, dragged the river bed with ropes. Someone dived into the water, over and over. Perhaps he should have gone down there, told them it was too late, put them out of their misery. Yes, perhaps he should have. He remained where he was, silent.

It was dusk by the time he got back to the cottage. He was stiff with cold by then, and starving. The rare warm sweetness of baking filled his nostrils. A chair scraped and mother came hurrying into the narrow hallway, her eyes dark.

'Oh, you're back! Come in, come in to the kitchen. We've been waiting.' Her hand clasped his wrist.

He stood in the doorway and saw father sat upright at the table, shaven for once, his hair combed, shining with brylcreem. And on the table, filled with blackberry jam, a perfectly round, sugar-iced birthday cake.

'Be sure to make a wish,' his mother said, lighting the candles.

'I'll be joining the airforce,' he replied.

*

He read about it in the papers a few days later, when he cycled over to Lewes to join up. 'Virginia Woolf Believed Dead', the headline said. In the bookshop he flicked through one of her novels, searching for something from the woman with whom he'd shared death. A secret message, perhaps, a conclusion. But none of it made sense. The words were all in a jumble. Shoving the book back on the shelf, he left, the angry jangle of the doorbell vibrating through the still space in his head.

It couldn't be helped, he told himself again. She had been too far away, and it was all so small.

The Accomplice

– Sara Keene –

I was bored. Arse-numbingly bored. So bored that I had given in to an urgent need to stretch out in my usual corner of the parlour and sleep. There was a sudden sharp and painful tug on my ear.

"That's not very nice of you, Miss A," I said, yawning.

"I am not happy," said Miss Austen.

I sat up and cocked my eyebrow in a way that usually put a smile onto her funny little pudding face. She was pulling at her hair, with unfortunate results, as she paced around the small, airless room and I could see that her pen and writing paper lay untouched at the bureau.

"It's no good," she said. "I cannot write today any more than I could yesterday, or the day before. I find myself quite uninspired by the people here, Pepper, and I think only of returning with all speed to Hampshire. May God forgive me, but I wish that my uncle's horrible disease would hasten towards its conclusion and release me from my duties."

"I don't think it'll be long before he pops his clogs," I said.

"I am sure you are right, as usual," she said. "And of course I do not wish him dead but this gloomy house has quite stifled my imagination."

"We could both do with some fresh air," I suggested, managing a hopeful wag of my tail.

She brightened. "Indeed, it is time for our afternoon walk and I have a surprise for you. I received intelligence recently that there is an interesting family in the next village with five daughters. Surely I might find subject matter there for a novel?"

"Sounds promising," I said. Would I never persuade her to write anything with some real action in it?

"I am invited to take tea with the family today and it seems they have a fondness for basset hounds so we are to go together."

At this, my spirits lifted very slightly. Perhaps there would be some excitement in it for me. Maybe even the chance to repeat the teamwork of our first novel.

An hour later, we arrived in a pretty village of no more than fifteen homes and a church. We stopped at a large white house, were shown into the parlour, and saw it was overflowing with women. I counted six of them, all either sewing or reading or chattering. I felt as if I had walked into an overpopulated birdcage and my ears quickly began to ache.

"My dears," twittered Ma Bennet, "may I introduce Miss Jane Austen who is staying with her aunt and uncle, Mr. and Mrs. Miller. We are honoured to entertain so celebrated a writer."

After she had introduced her five daughters, and they'd made the usual fuss over my ears and my appealing but lugubrious expression, I was largely ignored, so I crept under the table looking for cake crumbs among the petticoats while Mrs. Bennet chattered on.

Jane was on track to make a wonderful match and Elizabeth had received a proposal from a cousin that she really should have accepted as he was going to inherit the estate. As a consequence of her refusal they were all going to be thrown out through some peculiarity in the law that I did not understand, something about an N-tail. I lost interest. Anyone would have.

Elizabeth was not a bad-looker but not what you would call a great beauty – pert I would say. Miss A singled her out as the clever sister, settled herself on the sofa next to her and turned on the charm.

"I must insist that you tell me all about your cousin's proposal and Jane's expectations of marriage," she cried, in that god-awful phony way of hers. "For no story of romance between a young man and woman could ever be dull to me."

She was up to her tricks again. I was fond enough of her but not when she was in full research mode. We had been stuck in this god-forsaken part of Hertfordshire for six weeks now, waiting for the old guy to die, and I had had to listen to her endless moaning about her writer's block until I just wanted to bite her fat little ankles.

Elizabeth was not having any of it, though. You could tell she had seen right through Miss A.

"There is every likelihood of my boring you, were I to share the intimate details of my sister's courtship," she said. "And as for my cousin's proposal, there is nothing to be told. He and my friend Charlotte are already married and settled in Kent."

Then she clammed up.

I took stock. Jane was a real looker, with big liquid eyes in a heart-shaped face, but she was not chatty. Lydia was only interested in guys in uniform. Mary, the ugly one, was a pompous bore. She had read our first novel and had opinions on it that she wanted to share, loudly. Kitty had nothing to say for herself but giggled a great deal. Not one of them offered me cake and I soon grew tired of rummaging through the skirt folds. It was none too fresh down there either. We finally left just as I thought I'd have to make a break for it.

Miss A was very quiet and thoughtful that evening but the next day she was fizzing.

"Pepper," she said, "you are to be my eyes and ears again. I shall endeavour to place you within the Bennet household under the pretext that my poor uncle has developed an irrational dislike of you. They can hardly refuse to offer me this assistance when he is so ill and I fancy that Elizabeth was very taken with you. You will listen to their conversations and tell me everything, as you did with the Dashwoods."

I knew it was useless to kick up and, I admit it, I needed a project. Within a couple of days, I was installed at the Bennets, where I stuck like a burr to Elizabeth.

"Look how agreeable he is," she said to Jane shortly after my arrival, stroking my silky ears as I sat at her feet in the garden, giving her one of my cutest looks. "He shall be my constant companion." And so I was, but try as I might, I could not piece together a decent story.

After a week of making myself adorable and of having to concentrate instead of snoozing, I was taking a well-earned break and snuffling around in a corner of the kitchen garden when I was startled to sniff out Miss A who was loitering behind the raspberry canes, her bonnet askew and her skirt muddy.

"Pepper," she hissed. "Come here at once and tell me what you have learned." I trotted round to her side and told her what I knew. It did not take long.

"It won't suffice, Pepper," she said sadly. "My publisher has today written to tell me that he must have my new book before the end of the summer. It is already more than a year since the publication of 'Sense and Sensibility' and he fears that we will lose the loyalty of my readers."

I returned to the house, downcast and anxious, to discover that the world had somersaulted in the last hour. Jane's beau had left the neighbourhood, she was in shreds and going away somewhere to get some head space. Elizabeth had been invited to Kent to visit her friend

Charlotte and the apparently unbearable Mr. Collins and I was to go with her.

A few days later, we were there and I was wishing myself back in Hertfordshire. Mr. Collins was a creep and his dull household was surprisingly resistant to my charms. Far too often, I found myself banished to the outbuildings and spent many evenings alone while he, Elizabeth and the saintly Charlotte dined with a lonely old crone who lived in the grand house up the road. Elizabeth's least favourite person, Mr. Darcy, was staying there and she would return, seek me out and launch into an entertaining commentary on his rudeness as we sniffed around the garden in the fading light.

After a fortnight of this, my luck finally turned. Elizabeth and I were alone in the parlour, playing 'Find the Bone', when Mr. Darcy was announced. He and his snooty wolfhound stalked into the room. Neither of us was one bit prepared for what he'd come to say. To cut to the chase, he proposed to her. Who knew? But then she let him have it. It was a massacre. She said she would not marry him if he were the last man on earth, that he had behaved like a rat and that she could not stand his smug face…or words to that effect. Finally, he stormed out.

Elizabeth was shaking.

"Oh Pepper," she cried, hauling me onto her lap, "I cannot believe I spoke so boldly to him. I care not for his good opinion but I am shocked that he has so misjudged me as to think there was the slightest possibility that I might accept him."

This was a promising plot development but things soon improved even further. The next morning Elizabeth was walking me round the boundary of the old lady's estate when Mr. Darcy and Snooty came down the path. He thrust a letter into her hand, turned on his heel and left. She sat down on a tree trunk to read it. I watched her face turn bone-white and then flush a vivid pink. Actually, it suited her.

"Mr. Darcy has been the victim of a terrible misunderstanding, Pepper," she said. "He is not the wicked man I thought him and I have done him a great injustice."

I had no idea what she was talking about but I did not care. Surely, Miss A would have enough imagination to fill in the gaps. The next day we returned to Hertfordshire. Elizabeth was lost in thought the whole way. I couldn't wait to recount the new developments and was glad to spot Miss A lurking behind an oak tree as we neared the house. Elizabeth was too preoccupied to notice my absence as I scampered down the drive to pour out my story, carrying with me Mr. Darcy's letter, which I had pulled from her pocket.

Miss A looked terrible. She was without a bonnet and her hair was unkempt and dirty. She had a generally desperate and dishevelled air about her as if she had given up hope but she quickly rallied as I filled her in on recent events. When she read the letter, her eyes began to sparkle for the first time in months. I had to lift my leg on the tree to deal with the unexpected rush of relief. She did not notice the splash on her shoe.

"My dear Pepper," she said, "I am indebted to you forever. I do not think it necessary to prolong your stay with the Bennets, for my uncle passed away yesterday and we will shortly return to Hampshire. No doubt Miss Elizabeth Bennet will miss you but I wager she will shortly find herself inclined to accept Mr. Darcy's hand when he proposes again, as he surely must." I was so excited at the thought of going home that I spun in circles, barking wildly, until I tripped over my own ears and tumbled in a heap at her feet.

Miss A and I returned to Hampshire three days later. I was exhausted from my efforts and slept for a week, waking only to eat and drink and inhale the comforting smells of home. When I finally surfaced and made my way to the parlour, I found Miss A with a pile of paper covered in her spidery scrawl.

"It is well advanced, Pepper," she said. "I aim to deliver a happy outcome for Elizabeth and Mr. Darcy and for Jane and her beloved. Even poor foolish Lydia will find a measure of happiness. I am pleased with it. Let me read some of it to you."

I had to hand it to her – she was a speedy worker. She had taken the bones of the story, changed many of the details, invented new characters and the result so far was pretty good. Personally, I would have preferred a bit less talking and a bit more background detail but I thought it had a good chance of pleasing her readers. It just needed an arresting opening sentence and she had not found it yet. I thought for a moment and then something came to me that I had heard Elizabeth say to Jane one day.

"How's this?" I said. "It is a truth universally acknowledged that a single man in possession of a good fortune must be in want of a wife."

"Oh, Pepper," said Miss A with a happy sigh, picking up her pen. "It is not altogether fitting, but it will certainly suffice for now."

You can only do so much. I got up, stretched and went out into the garden in search of an old bone.

43

The End Of The Line

– Glenys Newton –

2015. The news was full of it. Refugees swarming onto our shores, banging on our front doors from Calais. 'It's getting closer,' screamed the media. 'It's alright we've spent millions on a really high fence,' our government reassured.

I found myself trying to imagine who these marauders could possibly be. How could they live in the middle of Calais with nothing? Surely this couldn't be true. The only way to find out was to go and see with my own eyes, and visit what is still commonly known as 'The Jungle'. I was driven by a sense of incredulity and fury that that this was happening just 90 miles from London. I set off with my son and my trusty van full of tents, sleeping bags and shoes.

Nothing could have prepared us for what greeted our eyes and senses. The Jungle in Calais is unique in that it has a huge mix of cultures, nationalities, religions and ethnicities all in one space. Most refugee camps are largely one nationality, say a Syrian refugee camp, but Calais has people from Kuwait, Afghanistan, Pakistan, Sudan, Kurdistan, Eritrea, Ethiopia, Syria, Iran, Iraq, Egypt, Kosovo, Albania, Palestine and different sub-cultures within those cultures. To us it felt like a mirror held up to the world. It felt like the very belly of hell, the result of all the worst things that man is capable of doing to his own kind.

We were unprepared for the utter squalor. Children playing on ground covered with raw sewage, flimsy tents doing little to keep out the elements, and mud, mud and more mud. More than anything we were unprepared for the generosity and beauty of the people who greeted us with broad smiles. Never in my life have I been treated with such kindness; people beckoned us over to give us tea and whatever little food they had, keen to tell their stories. People who had crossed deserts, seas and walked until their feet were raw. On the map, the little bit of water between Calais and Dover seemed nothing in comparison with the journeys already travelled. But at Calais they found themselves stuck, unable to go forwards, unable to go backwards. They had found themselves at the end of the line. As I listened to each story during my time there, my heart shattered.

A beautiful young girl from Sudan, 15 years old, in almost perfect English greeted me shyly. She wanted to practice her English and said that she had taught herself by watching English films and listening to music. She was there with her 5 year old sister who had that haunted look in her eyes that so many young children in The Jungle have. I pointed to her bandaged arm and she said that she had hurt it trying to get on the train that travels the Channel Tunnel. Each night, she tried to get on a train with her 5 year old sister. This little girl should have been wondering what was in her packed lunch for school, or what to make out of Lego, or what bedtime story she would like to hear; she should not have been risking death, trying to jump on a train each night to reach safety and her family.

I sat in the library for a whole afternoon with a 14 year old boy from Kurdistan. The library, Jungle Books, was a sanctuary. Once inside you could almost pretend that you were not sitting in the centre of Hades, and be nurtured by the calm of the books. We didn't share much common language but I did manage to understand that his brother is in England and he wanted to join him. We spent the whole afternoon playing noughts and crosses and games that didn't involve language but did involve a great deal of laughter. Laughter is the same in any language and I had never met people who were able to laugh so easily. Other people from Kurdistan began to gather in the library and we got an atlas out. They all began to show me where home was, to talk about home and how much they missed the beauty of the mountains – Zagros, Karokh, Hasarost, Bradost – the names of mountains that were their friends. One man looked wistfully at a map of the world and said that maybe there is a planet out there that has not yet been discovered, a planet where the Kurdish people are welcome because they are certainly not welcome on this one.

Another volunteer asked if I would help to take a husband and wife and their four year old daughter to a hotel. They had travelled from Iran and the wife had been heard crying, deep sobbing-crying, in the caravan where they were staying. Funds had been rallied to get them into a hotel, somewhere safe and warm even if it was just for one night. Their four year old daughter was autistic, blind and terrified. They had made the journey from Iran, in lorries, boats, and on trains with their four year old autistic, blind girl. I couldn't begin to imagine the terror that girl must have felt on that journey and then in the camp itself. The noise, smells and chaos of the camp were impossible to comprehend even when you could see what was going on. The parents also tried, on evenings when they could, to get into the back of a lorry with their little girl to get to England, to get to family. I took the husband in my car to the hotel and during the 20 minute journey I could not think of one single thing to say. How bad, exactly, did life have to get to consider leaving your home and your country, taking your blind autistic child with you, into the unknown? What on earth could I say to someone whose life had been reduced to that? All I could see were scars in their eyes. Wounds that went so deep there was no end. I saw pain, humiliation and fear but, worst of all, I could see the loss of hope. Not one glimmer. Isn't that what keeps us all going? Hope? Even the most tragic of stories has to have a thread of hope running through it. We all hope for things, to be safe, for our children to be safe but, for some people in the world, that hope isn't realistic. What kind of world turns its back on people longing to be safe, to stay alive? I saw scars in their eyes where that hope had been shattered.

I spent a few hours clearing rubbish from behind tents where families were living. A young six year old girl came to help me and we spent the time working quietly and solidly, sometimes exchanging a smile. We created our own little bubble of a world in that madness. Rats ran out from the rubbish and we just shrugged. I do not do well with rats but I couldn't show any disgust, fear or signs of cracking in the face of this beautiful, strong and wise-beyond-her-years girl. Without batting an eyelid she picked up maggots, old rice, shit, and dirty nappies, then we carried heavy bags, dripping with goodness-only-knows-what, out onto the main drag. With each bin bag filled and dispatched, we high-fived our success. It will be a lucky school that gets her in their class one day.

There was a centre for women and children but it was full up and the husbands were not allowed to be with their wives and children in the centre, a strictly women-only policy. There was a place available for teenage refugees in Calais but they only have four beds so it's not even worth asking. From what I can understand the law does not protect these young people, and to say that they are vulnerable in The Jungle is an understatement.

A man asked if I would be able to get him some more gas. He was in a caravan with his wife who was pregnant and six days overdue. 'Get some gas,' sounds simple. First find a spanner – so go through a field of about 400 people all asking for something, towards the people building shelters, find someone who has a spanner and is willing to lend it to you, then go back through the field of 400 people with yet more requests. Undo the gas bottle. Then find someone who is willing to give you the money for a new gas bottle. Drive out of the camp, running the gauntlet of the armed police, and then drive several miles and try to find somewhere that sells gas bottles, all the while following dubious instructions in French. Eureka! Somewhere that sells gas bottles. Buy one. Go back down the motorway and back through the crowd of armed police. Can't fit the gas bottle because it has a different regulator. Find someone who knows about regulators. Get told that there is someone up the other end of the camp which is a mile or so away. Walk down there, by which time word has spread that you were seen carrying a gas bottle and you receive about 300 requests for gas bottles. Find said person who is busy taking someone to hospital and asks can you come back later? A fight has broken out over a bicycle and a gentle, lovely Eritrean man approaches you with terror in his eyes. He says the sound of fighting reminds him of war, so you take him to the library where he feels safer. You are then stopped by a young Afghani man who'd given you tea the previous day. His cousin was killed last night on the train. Can you help him get his body back? He is afraid that the hospital will take his cousin's kidneys and organs. Find number of a hospital, find someone who has a phone so that you can ring the hospital, realise that your French definitely doesn't stretch to dealing with the morgue and find someone to interpret. By this time, you need to go back to the person who may have news about a regulator. Find him – hurray! He has a regulator – double hurray! He is going to fit it himself – sodding miracle. Have you fitted a carbon monoxide detector? he asks. Your eyes glaze over. You can't even begin to think how impossible it is to find a carbon monoxide detector. Manage to distract him long enough so that he fits the gas bottle. You suggest to the family that, for now, whenever they cook, they should keep the doors open in case they die. Ah yes, they laughingly reply. The pregnant lady is now getting twinges and by some sort of miracle you manage to track down a volunteer who is a trainee midwife. *Simply* fitting a gas bottle takes you nine hours.

On the last evening, I stood on a little hill with a young lad, the same age as my son. We stared at the full moon. I gave him a load of tobacco. He didn't smoke, it was for the tear gas. Apparently blowing tobacco smoke in people's eyes neutralises the tear gas, a nightly hazard while dodging the police. He told me that he was going to try and get on a lorry that night in another attempt to reach family in the UK. He was a surveying engineer but had to flee his country because of death threats. In his city 300,000 oil tanks left every day to be delivered to our shores, but his family had to live on charity given by the Americans since there was no food. The irony was not lost on him. He reminded me of my son and it broke my heart. He thanked me for my kindness over the past few days and I had absolutely no answer to give him. He was forced to flee violence that was carried out in my name and is continuing to be carried out in all of our names. He was stuck in the camp when I could just swan onto the ferry because I'd been lucky enough to be born in the right place. All I could do was to try and be the person that I'd hope my son would meet if he was ever away from home without family and needed help. It didn't feel very much but for that split second, staring at the moon, with this wonderful young man, it was everything.

Scalpelling Through

– Sarah Evans –

The moment comes, your body primed, one final wrenching push, a face-contorting scream.

It's done.

The baby rips from you.

'Well done, you!' Linda, the midwife, exclaims, as if you've brought about a miracle. Which, of course, you have.

Your birth-plan states that the baby should be placed directly on your stomach, and you wait for the first contact skin on skin. *Please may it be a girl.* Except you are trying not to hope too much. *A boy is fine too.* You sense the pause before you feel the sacks-of-sugar heaviness placed on the swell which has yet to deflate. Your fingertips touch the slippery birth gunge, its texture like cream-cheese. The air smells of blood, of amniotic fluid, of iodine. You wait for the surge of joy, of love, of something, but you're still waiting for the news. And even through the fug of pain and exhaustion you've registered that something is wrong.

'What is it? What's wrong with...' You lack the pronoun.

'Everything's absolutely fine,' Linda says. She's trying too hard to smile and you know that she's lying. 'It's a healthy baby...'

One of the nurses comes close. 'Dr Sanders is on his way,' she whispers, but loud enough that you hear.

Your baby's skin is purple-blue. Black strands of hair are plastered against the skull. The face looks squashed from this angle. Eyes closed.

Lips puckering. Implausibly tiny nose. The body is splayed over yours, like a frog. And still no one has told you: boy or girl.

The night passes darkly, second by time-stop second; it's terror – not exhilaration – keeping you awake. You worried about so many things. Sticking to your five-a-day and lots of calcium. Avoiding alcohol and second-hand smoke. You even – God help you – played Mozart. You worried about the development of strong heart and lungs. About breech births and obstructed labour. You read up on syndromes, particularly *in view of your age*. The scans showed everything was fine; it wasn't unusual for gender to be unclear.

Your phone glows: *3am*. There is no one to call. No partner. No parents. Mostly you have social media friends in lieu of real ones.

You re-examine events, how it was you convinced yourself to go ahead with this unlikely thing, remembering the drunken pursuit of pleasure, the carelessness and subsequent irresolution. Perhaps a child would fix your life in place, anchor the drifting. The fault must be yours, you know that, lying within your flawed reasoning.

The cot lies close. By the dim nightlight, miniature fingers fist tight, framing the sleeping face which you search for clues. But the baby looks like a baby, facial features holding their secrets close.

The doctor uses technical terms and quickly you lose track. You stare down at your ragged nails and wait for the moment he will stop talking problems, cutting through the jargon to his answers, the happy future conjured out of the citrus-scented air. 'So,' he says. 'To summarise...'

He holds up four fingers. The dimensions of gender. Up until now you pretty much thought there was only one. *Boy or girl*. Surely it was that simple.

Biology is more adaptable than you ever imagined. Penises; clitorises; scrotums; labia: these all exist on a spectrum of size and morphology. Nature cannot always make up her mind.

Earlier a nurse came round to demonstrate nappy changing and bathing. You sank back into the pillow and refused to open your eyes. It wasn't so much the baby that you couldn't bear to see, but the look on the nurse's face. Revulsion. Pity. Disapproval.

The doctor's screen is filled with a black-white image. Internal sex organs are not clear cut either.

A blood test reveals the chromosomes and you remember GCSE biology. XX for girl. XY for boy. No one said how different cells might tell different stories.

The fourth component is psychological; it is all in the mind.

Nature can't decide, but ultimately your child will know. You've heard of transgender of course, but never really understood what it meant, how that could even be possible, always thought it was some mixed up, freaky thing.

The factors are finely balanced.

'You mean we have to wait years? Before anyone can know?'

Dr Sanders smiles, a sympathy-laden smile. 'Not exactly.' Responsible adults must step in, assigning a provisional label that the child might later reject.

Boy or girl. You remember longing for the power to select. You never imagined your wish coming true. Boy or girl. *You* decide.

You try to adapt to your new circumstance. Newly a mother. Freshly aware of how complex life can be.

You always believed that you would be tolerant of sexuality. Of lifestyle choices and belief systems. That love would be unconditional.

Duty kicks in and your baby is kept fed, clean and safe. You are brusquely efficient when it comes to changing nappies.

You gaze down at your child and unfocused eyes stare back. Dr Sanders advised that selecting gender would help you connect with your baby. You try names out loud, as if this might hold the key. 'Chloe? Scarlett?' Surely a girl would feel less alien. 'Oscar?' Is it harder to be a sissy than a tomboy? The baby's head turns sideways. Limbs flap uncoordinatedly. 'Ashley? Jayden?' Those feel a cop out. The baby's face begins to pucker, at the ready to cry.

You pick the baby up, tension threading through the small body, the cries developing into full throttled despair. '*Shush* now, *shush.*' Your voice does not provide soothing. Saliva dribbles down, soaking into the duckling-yellow baby-grow. You pace the small room which you painted jade. '*Shush* now.' Nothing you have bought is pink or blue, partly because you didn't know, but in any case you despised the idea of colour-coding from such a tender age. You'd intended to buy your baby both dolls and cars. You would encourage a girl to be adventurous and teach a boy to play gently.

You were determined your child would not be defined and limited by their sex.

You hear the knocking at the door and your heart is hammering too. The two of you are locked in the bathroom. *Go away. Go away.* You wait an eternity before emerging.

The health visitor has left a card. You picture all her questions – *and how are you coping?* – and her wanting to measure your naked baby's weight.

Please ring to rearrange.

You ponder what will happen if you ignore it. Some tiny, detestable part of you wonders if it might not be simpler if the baby were taken away. *Problem solved!*

You open the fridge and shuffle the condiments. The freezer is reduced to the Balti pizzas you had a craving for during pregnancy and which you cannot stomach now. For eight days you have not stepped outside, telling yourself that you will feel stronger tomorrow.

You peer through the window into a grey world.

You have to do this eventually.

The baby is oil and talcum-powder fresh. You lay the small body down in the pram which you bought with such optimism. Mittened hands wave. You wrap yourself up, enveloping your stale sweat and sour-milk smell in the protective bulk of padded clothing. Opening the door triggers a pull-back fear and stepping outside feels like entering a cold, rough sea. You look left then right, on the lookout for neighbours you barely say *hello* to. But you've seen before, how people peer and coo at babies, claiming them as public property.

You keep your head down and the hood of your hoodie up. Walking briskly, your legs quickly tire, as if your life-force has been drained by this tiny being who looks so beatific in sleep. You can't – simply cannot – nip into the corner shop, the one where the owner recognises you and asked about your due date.

You carry on up the hill to the small supermarket.

The logistics of opening doors one handed and manoeuvring yourself plus pram inside nearly defeat you. The baked-goods scent is cloying, the air chill from the fridges, though not enough to account for the way you freeze in front of the nappies, all those images of blissfully happy mother-baby pairs.

Coordinating   the   pram,   navigating   narrow   aisles   whilst simultaneously carrying a basket... intent on concentrating, you fail to be sufficiently alert.

'Kirsty!'

Hearing your name startles you out of all proportion. You look round, desperately hoping there is another Kirsty.

Lucy. From work. Her smile is not for you, it is for your baby. She gushes words, they foam and spew and your heart is thumping so hard in your ears that you can scarcely hear.

Yes, you force yourself to say, the birth went OK, though *OK* strikes you as an odd way to describe your body being rent in two.

Sorry, you say, for not being in touch, just that you have been so busy. *Busy* is not right either, not for your inert shock.

Yes, you say, you and the baby are fine. You feel conscious of your unwashed hair, as if that might account for your discomfiture.

And then, there it is, the cut to the chase, the obvious question together with the smiling expectation that whatever binary answer you give, Lucy's response can remain the same. *How lovely.*

You turn to stone. You don't have the answer and giving a provisional one would leave you feeling bound. It's not the kind of mix-up you could explain.

The moment lingers, intolerably long. The smile wanes, replaced by a crease of puzzlement between Lucy's eyes.

'I'm sorry,' you say. You mumble something about needing air, and already you are turning the pram around, knocking against shelves and triggering expletives from the man whose ankles you ram into. You drop the half-full basket and force your way through the entry-only door and then you are outside, face flushed hot, and you are running down the hill, some mad-arse mother with a pram that is veering out of control.

*

You brace yourself against instinctive distaste and take to Googling and watching YouTube, sieving rivers of information, looking for an answer that makes sense.

People share such intimate things. They talk about surgery, performed in a time before memory. *Cut now and don't ask about what happens later.* You cross your legs and wince. They talk of appalling experiences at school. Of disownment by families. Of being pushed into being one thing only to discover themselves to be something else. Of secrets kept from them, the relief of discovery and understanding clicking into place. They talk about how to broach things with a potential date. About painful rejections. They have medical problems. Fertility problems. Psychological problems.

And some talk about chancing upon acceptance and happiness.

The tug of disappointment threatens to pull you down and under. You were hoping to hear that the doctor had it wrong, that there were solutions which could be implemented here and now.

You dally over an onscreen image, unable to discern gender. The hair is straight, feathered slightly around the face, longer than the male norm but by no means unusual. Cheekbones prominent. No Adam's apple or five o'clock shadow. No makeup. No jewellery. You press *play*.

'My name is Chris,' the person says, the voice mid-pitch.

You watch more than you listen, trying to figure it out, the ambivalence disconcerting. Like one of those optical illusions, you'd see it if you were told. This person likes to use his or her hands to add emphasis. Fingers are longish for a woman, but not particularly mannish. A guitar player's hands. Everything appears indeterminate. Mid-way.

The person smiles, the expression neither feminine nor masculine, just an asymmetric curl of amusement.

61

'You want to know what I decided?' the Chris person says. The shrug is off-hand, as if the answer is obvious. 'I decided to be me.'

The room smells of institution. The woman writes down your answers.

'Jess,' you say. 'No, it isn't short for anything.'

The moment comes. You are fully primed, yet her question catches you off-balance. 'Gender?'

You are free to give the answer that you choose. Any answer but the truth.

The registrar's smooth expression wavers as she senses the not-rightness to your faltering. She's expecting a straightforward reply. At your side, the baby's gaze is wide-eyed and curious, so fully human. Possible futures hover on your pause. You push yourself to deliver your prepared response.

'Girl.'

The word rips from you, cutting through the sterile air; it is written down, legally defining things.

'What a beautiful baby,' the registrar says and smiles her part-of-the-job smile.

'Yes.' And likely it's only you who notices the hesitation. '*She* is.'

It is done.

For now.

Room Service

- Claudine Toutoungi -

I am an actor. I am playing the role of an airport hotel cleaner. I am playing the role, but that is not who I am. Watch me as I glide the duster over the trouser-press. See how I hoover the room. Aren't I convincing? When I polish the mirror, it will really look like I am polishing the mirror. The same when I tidy shampoo packets into piles.

This hotel has cigarette-burns in the carpet and sirens outside. It's full of sad men in suits, smelling of planes. Their eyes droop. The sag they leave in the bed stays sagged. This one's been here for ten days. It's a long time for an airport hotel stay, but I don't ask. In the mornings his pillows are wet with tears. I ignore them. I am not even a real cleaner, so what's it to me?

By the way, if I get my words wrong, that's your fault. I am fluent in three languages but this one lays traps to trip you up. Take 'I wiped the floor with him'. I know what that means. It isn't anything to do with cleaning. I learn these phrases but I never practise them. My only friends here are *Haze, Jif* and *Mr.Muscle* and they don't say much. Anyway that suits me fine. They don't have a problem with how I spend my hours. How do I spend my hours? I spend them dancing.

The dance needs sun and space to do it properly. Here the sky has a black belly and my life is in hotel rooms. Still I can dance to the berimbau in my head, pouring bleach down the fourteenth dirty toilet-bowl, I can dance as I scrub the fourteenth dirty toilet bowl. I can even dance as the businessman comes into the bathroom, watches me for ten minutes, then says, 'Funny job for a bloke' and walks out.

At night, I walk home by a long stretch of river. You can see it's bad water, brown water, the kind that drags you down so I don't let it into my head, don't let it mix with the ocean I grew up next to. Once I'm home, I drink six beers. Then I cook two eggs. I peel the shell away from the soft flesh and eat one of them. Put the other in my pocket. I like its weight. Sweet egg. Like it's nesting.

It's good to hide my dancing behind sweeping and wiping. It's good because the dance, like me, is also in disguise. Always has been. It makes me happy to know this, so I hum, which is when, the businessman comes in again, to see me mopping the floor.

'I won't disturb you'.

He stands in front of me.

'Left a bit.' He points to a corner. I mop it. It's clean but I let him see me mop it again.

'Thank you,' he says.

His eyes are red. I don't ask why.

'Fancy a cig?'

I shake my head. He lights a cigarette. Starts to smoke. My eyes avoid the sign that says no-smoking.

'What about the toilet?'

He points to the toilet I've already cleaned. He sees me looking.

'Done it?' he says.

I nod.

'How about you do it again? How about you do it, so I don't complain?'

I smile, set down my mop, pick up the bleach. I go over to the toilet, open it, pour it in. When I reach out for the toilet-brush, he puts his hand in the way. He does it deliberately. I stare at his arm. It has a mole the shape of Rio on it. Then he shifts forward. He's reaching to take my face in his hands. 'Come here,' he says.

I turn him over with my dancing arm. He is on the floor hard and in pain and I have mashed the egg in my pocket. He moans. I have given away my secret. The dance that is not a dance. All those pretty movements always in my head – attack, defence, attack, defence. It's out the bag and I should care, but I don't. The dance is a fight and it always has been a fight.

'I am not a cleaner,' I tell him and I turn my pocket inside out. Bits of egg rain down on his face. The noise he makes is sad. 'Egg on your face,' I say. Then I put my *Haze* and my *Jif* and *Mr.Muscle* on my trolley, and whistling, I wheel them out the door.

Calentitos

– Deborah Arnander –

Don Emilio strokes the razor blade against his cheek and thinks about Carmela. Carmela's eyes are deep as wells. He never likes to look in them too long: a man might drown himself. Other days they seem all surface, lacquer-hard. When she turns the wheel of batter in the spitting fat she narrows them to slits.

It was by her eyes he knew her first. They are unchanged, in her changed face. He spoke his order, she inclined her head. He watched her disappear inside, the apron neatly tied around her waist, her hair in its tight bun all streaked with grey. In three years since, she's given not a single hint that she remembers him. She treats him with the same diffident courtesy she shows to all her customers.

He curses God beneath his breath: a drip of blood is rolling down his chin. It splashes, scarlet on the white. A sign of vigour, that his blood still flows so readily. A nuisance too. The *muchacha* has starched the collar of his best blue shirt, which must remain immaculate.

He finds a pad of gauze inside the cabinet. Pressing it against the wound he feels his hand is trembling. At his age, he should not have to shave himself, but what is the alternative? The first and last time he sat in the new barber's chair, he felt the young man hesitate deliberately, blade poised at Don Emilio's throat. The barber caught his eye and smirked. In the background Don Emilio could see the apprentice girl, distracted from the clumps of hair around her feet, and gawping like

71

a witness to a martyrdom. When the barber had done, he slapped cologne on Don Emilio's cheeks. Holding Don Emilio's head between his hands, the barber pursed his lips, as though about to plant a kiss. He tittered when Don Emilio squirmed, which he should not have done. Don Emilio feels the heat rise to his neck now with the shame of it.

The bleeding took its time to stop, and Don Emilio is several minutes late. As he hurries underneath the arch his left foot skids out on the stones; he totters, flounders, manages to right himself. He pictures his grandfather's silver-handled cane, which Miguel, his chauffeur, has unearthed and placed in the umbrella stand. When Miguel hands Don Emilio out of the car, he leans in far enough to give him the correct support, passes him his newspaper only when he's had a chance to catch his breath. He must admit that he is lucky, with Miguel.

Perhaps Miguel is right, and it is time... But glancing back, he notices a slick of candlewax, left on the cobblestones from the processions a month ago. So his infirmity is not to blame. Like most of the humble people in this town, the street sweepers have grown lazy. Famished, shoeless children, whom Don Emilio remembers whimpering for crumbs: now they have children and grandchildren of their own, who pass by Don Emilio's door on their way home from school, send cans of Fanta bouncing down the street, scatter the wrappings of their American-style snacks. Many are grotesquely fat. The *muchacha*, too, is barrel-shaped, her housecoat biting underneath her arms. The *muchacha* is saving money for her wedding to her *novio*. If Don Emilio speaks to her she lifts her eyes to his: he sees the shadows of her calculations pass across her face. She would like to move him to pity, or even to affection. Devoid of subtlety, she merely irritates. He is irritated, thinking of her now, and irritated with himself for putting up with her too long, it is time that he replaced her, he will see to it on his return.

His mouth begins to water at the smell that drifts across the colonnaded square: that smell of tender dough plunged into boiling oil, so familiar from childhood. Carmela's *calentitos* are as good as Inés's were: the skill must be inbred. He is pleased to see his table is unoccupied. The locals know his habits, but there are many tourists since the opening of the hotel. White linen, *platos del pueblo*, blackened paintings from the flea market, and young Gavira, with his greased hair and his quilted jacket, kissing hands, clicking his heels. A few of the foreigners, from Germany, Denmark, England, countries with no sunlight of their own, have bought property here. They favour the rotting *palacios* with stone blazons above their doors. Like his neighbour, the Englishwoman, who even now is trundling across the square. She raises her arm in greeting; he makes a little bow. The Germans stay only for the holidays, and bring all their food from Germany, in tins. But the Englishwoman is a fixture, engaging everyone in her execrable Castilian. She has swollen legs and a face like a sad elephant. Don Emilio has watched her puzzling over the marble plaque on the front wall of his house; when she speaks to him he pretends not to hear. There are reports she's friendly with the homosexual who runs the antiques shop. Don Emilio has also heard she drinks the water from her well, which dates from Roman times. Nobody has told her what is down that well. It will make her sick before too long.

Carmela comes towards him, carrying his tray. He studies the movements of her wrists as she lowers the tray onto the table, sets out the cup of coffee and the basket of cooling *calentitos* with its lining of fresh paper. It is his pleasure and regret to watch her walk away, and to appreciate the still-neat lines of her, the slender ankles, the fine calves, the narrow waist with its white bow — she looks just like her mother from the back; the only sign that she's approaching sixty is the slight stoop of her shoulders. Facially, she favours her father: serious, with those huge black eyes in which you see yourself reflected. Inés had a broad face, plump cheeks despite her slender frame; she was gay as a bird, always singing around the house. Here she is, smiling as she strips the sheet off his bed. *It is nature,* with that little shrug. He has never seen Carmela gay like that. It occurs to him he's never heard her laugh. What became of her, in her years away? She left the convent before she had to take her vows, came back after forty years and bought the café: that is all he knows. There is a tight point like a stitch in his right lung; perhaps it is a punishment because he let Inés come in. To fortify himself he calls to mind the day he and Papa accompanied the General. As they make their way towards the best seats in the shade, people cringe and press their backs against the walls, attempting to incrust themselves. He draws on it, that power, he tastes it on his tongue. Opening his eyes he checks the *calentitos,* which are, as always, irreproachable: smooth and brown and even, as though healthily suntanned.

Ah. Always the first bite is the best. The crisp skin yields between the teeth, then fragrant steam coils from the hollow at the *calentito*'s heart. It's like a warm breath in his mouth. Carmela uses fresh oil every day; he loves to watch her pull and guide the dough with her long sticks. The secret is to get the thickness right, to keep the spiral fine, with just a tiny portion in the centre that's a little fatter than the rest, and provides the refinement of contrast. Carmela's are not *churros,* such as you get in the capital, all soft and greasy, their insides like mashed potato; these are genuine *calentitos de rueda,* made the traditional way. Don Emilio has heard that *calentitos* come from China, via Portugal. It was a jealously guarded secret, the method of their manufacture: the Emperor imposed the death penalty on those caught sharing it with foreigners.

The Englishwoman has detained Carmela with her usual one-sided conversation. When she does not know a word, she hesitates and casts about, apparently unconscious of the time this wastes. Alerted by her voice, the ugly stray known as Pepe appears, stopping for a second in its tracks to scratch the fleas around its neck. It settles at the Englishwoman's feet, its great head resting on its short front legs, and every now and then looks up at her with white-ringed eyes. Carmela is standing at some distance from the Englishwoman's table, her body half turned towards the kitchen: there are *tortillas* to prepare for lunch. Carmela shifts her weight, moves the empty tray from one hand to the other, taps it briefly against her hip. There she stands, radiating signs: signs Don Emilio can clearly read, and the foreigner, in her ignorance, her selfishness, cannot. He pushes the basket of *calentitos* aside.

The Englishwoman, he gathers, is giving her opinion of last month's *novena*. In Don Emilio's house this feast has never been a cause for celebration: *braceros* drunk for nine long days, deliberately trampling his family's fields, which lie between the shrine and the walls of the town, and which, for centuries, the humble people have had permission to pass through for the duration of the festival. Carmela's attention hangs by the thinnest of threads – he can almost see it, slackening in the air - but the Englishwoman is determined to rehearse what she has learned, as though speaking to a fellow intellectual, whereas Carmela has had no schooling in her life, unless you count the nuns, and really you cannot. This story in any case is one Carmela knows: the history of the *patrona*, her discovery by a shepherd in a cave, at the time of the

Barbarians.

'Maria de Gracia, like you,' says the Englishwoman, holding out her palm, as though to encourage in Carmela the naïve belief that this coincidence entails some special sympathy between the *patrona* and herself.

Guiri, it is not even her name, Don Emilio tells the Englishwoman silently, it is how the nuns re-christened her: Carmela, Carmela, Carmela, this is her name, inside my mouth, and I know it and you do not.

Carmela smiles at the Englishwoman then. A smile that makes her eyes shine; a fond smile, as one would give a child. In her hoarse voice, Carmela says: 'It is the name of half the girls born in this town.'

She touches the Englishwoman's shoulder with her fingertips, and turns back to the kitchen.

Don Emilio lifts his chin, straightens his spine. The nuns were sentimental fools: not one of those they took remained. These days the sisters have to get black girls from Africa; a new one arrived the other day. Don Emilio has seen her in the street, walking round-eyed and bewildered in her thick brown robe; he has heard that when the sisters gave her a special treat, a plate of prawns, she started weeping, thinking they were grubs.

A picture comes, from childhood: the *patrona* floats towards him in a blaze of lights. He stares down from the balcony at her approaching face, rouged for the festival, her flat blue eyes, remote and pitiless, the glint of flames reflected in her stiff, encrusted gown. She is very old, the *patrona*, much older than the baroque virgins of the eighteenth century, who are as pretty as shop window mannequins, or the modern copies with their piteous expressions, their cascading tears; the *patrona* has nothing to inflame the men, no-one screams obscenities to praise her beauty when they gather around her shrine. She does not pander to the women, either, or presume to express their suffering. She is indifferent and she endures.

He shakes out the newspaper he has brought. He sees there is a new petition from the families. For one second he admits Inés, and the sound made by Domingo's spade as it at last removes her head; well, she is too long for the hole they've dug, and Papa is insisting that there isn't time. He takes a mouthful of the good coffee Carmela serves. So where do they propose to put them, since the cemeteries are full? In any case these people were not Christians. Still there are always those who want to stir the embers, reignite the fires. And thanks to them, old grievances persist. It is unfortunate.

Still Life

– Danusia Iwaszko –

When do you stop caring about people? When is the moment you have to say enough's enough, I can do no more for that person? I have two children and they're always saying that their friends wished they had a mum like me. Giving, giving, and taking that's what it's all about. I try my best.

'The train standing on platform 2 is the 10.10 to Orpington.'

That's the train I catch to work, or used to before ...

I didn't want to get a job but when Robert left us... the money has to keep coming in and the boys understand. They're young, it seems normal to them. I looked for a job near home, I didn't want to commute, no, I definitely didn't want to commute.

Why's that man staring at me? I get a little self conscious when men look at me but, on the other hand, I quite like being looked at. I'd never let on that I like it though. I mean, it has all sorts of connotations about being an object and us women have fought long and hard, Emily Pankhurst and all that, to get away from being objects, but secretly, I quite like being looked at - who doesn't? - as long as it's admiringly. Oh no he's moving towards me. As long as he doesn't touch me, that's the absolute limit. They do you know. Being looked at is one thing but being pawed is quite another. People react to me as if I were a statue, but why would there be a statue on Brixton station of all places? I want to move away. Move away then! 'Move! Move!'

'The train now standing on platform 5 is being prepared for service. Please do not board.'

I used to get dressed up for Robert, you know what I mean? Not the sort of dressed up you get for dinner parties, although I did that as well. I mean the other sort of dressed up. Robert used to like me in short skirts and fishnets and....Oh, dear, now I'm getting very embarrassed. Robert used to like to go out with me dressed like that but if other men looked at me he went berserk. It led to scenes. There's no pleasing some people. There was certainly no pleasing Robert... I wonder what luck his new woman's having?

Do you know why he fell for her? Do you know? Because she buys really expensive shoes; she thinks nothing of paying £100 or £150 for a pair of shoes and he thought this was wonderful. I can just imagine the scene if I had spent half that on a pair of shoes, not that I would have dreamt of doing such a thing. I pride myself on my thrifty home management. £150! That's what I spend on the entire month's groceries and if, only IF, there is a little left over then I buy myself a little treat and I don't feel too guilty.

The job I eventually found was for Mrs. Rasmussin. She's very elderly, Mrs. Rasmussin, but she has amazing energy for her age. My job is to do spot of cleaning. She doesn't like me to touch anything in the room where she paints though. I'd love to get my hands on it. It's so dusty and disordered and the bookcase with her art books in is filthy, but she says it's her space - her space, how lovely - so obviously, I don't intrude. She is quite brusque and domineering but it's just her way, she doesn't mean anything by it. 'I'll have a tea,' she commands, sitting in her Louis the Fourteenth chair. Everything has to be just so: the position of the glass on the tray in its silver holder, a slice of lemon on a little dish, a white lace doily. She's royal, you know, minor royalty from Eastern Europe, but royalty nevertheless. She's used to having things done for her. She says that the world is made up of two groups of people: people that do and people that have things done for them. Two completely different species, she says, but each totally dependent on the other. She says that it's nothing to do with class, or education, or money; it's to do with attitude. Mrs. Rasmussin says that's why Robert and I didn't work out. I liked to do things and he liked to get a chappy in to do it. Like the garden. I love doing the garden, the smells, the colours of the flowers, the sense of satisfaction at the end of the day. Robert said that we should have someone in to do it. I couldn't see the point, for me that defeats the whole object.

One summer I grew sunflowers, just for a laugh really, to see how tall they grew. The boys and I fell in love with them, those huge funny faces, their heads turned up to the sky. They really do follow the sun. We used to sing:

'For the heart that has truly loved never forgets,

But as truly loves on to the close,

As the sunflower turns to her God when he sets

The same look which she turned when he rose.'

'Let me out! I want to get out of here! Help! Somebody help me!'

They can't hear me of course, I realise that now. I kid myself sometimes that some very sensitive souls can hear me, but it's all a fiction.

'Somebody help me, please!'

No... They're all just piling on the train.

Funny how some people are so desperate to get onto a train they can't let the other passengers off first. I have come to the conclusion that those types that barge on are genuinely frightened that they will be denied their journey, but they won't be.

I used to like to catch the 3.04 home, to be back in time to make the boys their tea. My children eat horrible things. All they want is fish fingers, oven chips or their particular favourite, those potato letters, covered in batter. They delight in spelling out their names, finding a T, finding an O … I remember one day I was playing around with the letters when I spelt out L.O.N.E.L.Y.. It was such a shock! I'm not lonely, I'm too busy to be lonely with two children and a husband to look after. Husband, my husband. I love hearing people use that word. 'Will your husband be coming too?' I feel so grown up. My husband. Husband and wife. Two different roles. Him, going out into the world foraging and then returning to me in the home. I never questioned it, I never thought anything was wrong. Nothing was wrong.

Then last summer he started coming back from work later and later, with flowers. He would apologize for being late, asked me if I wanted a hand with the washing up. The feeling between us had shifted from comfortable unawareness to politeness. At first I was delighted, but gradually he started making comments about my behaviour. He said that he found my laugh irritating. We've been married nine years and he's never said anything about my laugh before. I felt this tension between us, but I never mentioned it, I thought it better to let sleeping dogs lie. Of course I had no idea that that sleeping dog was lying with my husband.

He told me one day, sitting in the back garden after dinner. I was watching the boys running about on the lawn, when Robert said, 'There's something I have to tell you.' He was looking down at his wine, swishing it around in the glass, 'I've met someone else.' The garden started to move before my eyes, the boys, the tall trees, Robert's face, the house, all gently spinning around me. The boys, Robert, the trees, the house. Boys, Robert, trees, house, boys, trees, boys, trees, boys, boys, boys...

When I came round I focused on the faces peering down at me. The boys were screaming. 'She's alright, she's alright,' Robert was saying. He lifted me back onto the white wrought iron chair. 'It's just the heat,' he said. The boys both clambered onto my lap and clutched me tight. I held onto them for dear life.

It was all practicalities after that. We dealt with it in a very civilized and British way. He moved out pretty soon afterwards, to a flat nearby that he'd purchased some months before.

We see each other regularly. Not so much though since I've been here. He's very supportive when it comes to the boys. He looked after them every other weekend when we split but my hours at Mrs. Rasmussin's increased, so he had to meet the boys after school, which I know isn't very convenient for him, but it's very difficult to say no to Mrs. Rasmussin.

You see, after I had been working for her for a couple of months she wanted to paint my portrait. I had to finish my chores and the sitting started quite late in the afternoon when it was really my time to go. I couldn't just stand up and walk out. Robert used to get very angry, 'Tell her you have to pick up the boys', but I couldn't. It was very important to her. This was a complete departure for her. She had never painted a portrait before, her area being landscapes and still life, but she said she thought she could tackle me.

One daren't move a muscle when Mrs. Rasmussin is painting you. I love the stillness that descends on the room, the complete concentration. The peace. Not perfect peace. Little noises, distant traffic, the occasional voice outside, but the room feels still. Stillness. I experienced stillness, maybe for the first time in my life.

I have long periods of stillness now, where nothing much happens, and I'm not uncomfortable with silences anymore. There, in Mrs. Rasmussin's room, I revisited my life. My childhood, my sister. I had always thought we were so close. I remembered us sleeping in the same room and playing together in this little dinghy we used to take on holiday, I recalled my excitement and my jealousy when she went out on her first proper date, and then underneath it all I started to feel this huge gap. This distance between us. Emptiness. I wept. Were we close? We were too scared, scared of what?

I used to look forward to my portrait sittings. I would choose a memory, an event from my past and revisit it. It was always the same. The way I remembered behaving and how I truly felt, rarely tallied. I recalled my father's funeral. I had shown the appropriate grief at the time. I had been dignified, had looked after my mother, but as I revisited the event I realised that I was none of these things. I was a little girl, frightened, confused and angry. I started to lay the picture of this little cowering girl over the controlled, capable woman. The true picture was a mess, a shock, a lie.

I started to see myself with my friends, I spent time with them all, even though they weren't there. Some of them I loved and some of them bored me rigid. But the most disturbing thing was that some of them gave me nothing at all. There, in that little room, I met them all again and I met them for the first time. Until then, life had been so busy, so full of activity, events had just rushed by. Now I returned in slow motion. I was away from my life and really close to it. Now that I was motionless, I was moved.

Oh no, there's a man coming towards me. I wish I could walk away from him but I can't anymore. This all happened very slowly but it happened all at once as well. After a few weeks of sitting for Mrs. Rasmussin I started to feel very tired. I had pains. Aches and pains. As I did the chores my legs would hurt. I started to find it difficult to walk. I thought I had one of those funny illnesses you hear of, M.E. M.S.. I kept being late for Mrs. Rasmussin. The amount of cleaning I did became less and less. She would get very angry, so would Robert. 'You have to shake off this depression,' he would say. The strange thing is I didn't feel depressed. My body was slowing down but somewhere deep down inside of me, out of my stillness, I was coming alive.

One day I was waiting here for my train to go to work. It pulled in, every one else got on but I couldn't. I just stood here. I had stopped. Stopped next to the tracks. Look at me, I'm a work of art.

The Second First Time

– Dani Redd –

Andy had spent his Sunday afternoon planning a year eight biology class. The deep sea, he'd tell them, is a place where no light penetrates. The pressure is immense, the water freezing. Then he'd show them pictures of deep-sea creatures – animals with transparent bodies, mystery squid with arms like cooked spaghetti – and they'd stare at him enraptured, not a phone in sight.

The front door opened and he heard footsteps on the stairs.

'Andy, are you in the study?'

'Yes!'

Cleo came in. Even though she'd piled her dark curls up on top of her head like a pineapple and was wearing the long lacy skirt that got caught on the door handles, she still looked beautiful.

'How was your afternoon?' he asked.

'Oh, it was so great. Silver Moon had a revirginisation ceremony! She was dressed all in white, like a bride, but it was as if she was only marrying herself,' Chloe said, eyes blazing with enthusiasm.

'That's pretty narcissistic. Classic Moon.'

Cleo narrowed her eyes.

'So, what exactly does this ceremony entail?' he asked hastily.

'It was amazing! There was a singing bowl meditation and everything, but it's more about what went on before. She literally had an operation to make herself a virgin again – she had her hymen stitched back together.'

He laughed. 'Out of all the ridiculous things she's done...'

There was no reply. He looked up at Cleo, and much to his distress saw tears in her eyes.

'What's wrong?'

'You don't understand anything!' she sobbed, rushing from the room.

He found her in the bedroom, a quaking lump under the duvet, and sat down next to her.

'Come on, come out. I'm sorry I insulted your friend.'

'You always do. It's not that.'

'Oh. Well I'm sorry I took the piss out of the ceremony. It just sounds, well, a bit silly.'

She pulled down the duvet, revealing a pair of hostile green eyes, red-rimmed from crying. 'And what makes you think that?'

'Getting a new hymen doesn't stop you from already having lost your virginity. And hymens don't just break during sex. They can break from using a tampon and from heavy exercise. Some women don't even have them.'

'You're mansplaining again.'

'Well you did ask,' he said irritably, and immediately wished he hadn't. The last thing he wanted was an argument. Whenever she was upset it affected him too, as if her sadness were contagious.

He stood up. 'Look, you're upset and I'm not helping. Shall we can talk about this later?'

She took his hand, and pulled him back towards her. 'I'm going to get revirginised too.'

'What?'

Surely she wasn't serious? Cleo had always been dead set against cosmetic surgery, but perhaps she didn't consider this as such.

'It's my body.' She rolled onto her side, away from him.

'Of course it is. But why the need for this?'

'Before I was ready to give it away, something was taken from me. Now I want it back.'

Her voice sounded distant, as if she'd fallen into the ocean and was drifting slowly downwards; through the thermocline and then the bathypelagic layer to the place where no light reached.

The walls and the ceiling were white. Cleo's hand, draped across her midriff, was almost as pale as the bed-sheets. She hadn't eaten or drunk anything all day and the lack of food combined with the anaesthetic was making her dizzy and dry-mouthed, as if she were marooned on a boat, way out at sea.

She remembered that party almost two decades ago where that boy had poured her vodka and cokes so strong they burned, and she hadn't complained because that's how alcohol was supposed to taste. Half an hour later she'd had to grip onto his shoulder for support because the room was spinning and her legs felt too limp to hold her weight. He'd taken her upstairs to someone's bedroom. And then he'd kissed her and she'd kissed him back without protesting because everyone knows that's what girls and boys are supposed to do. In the nights preceding this moment, whilst alone in her bedroom, she had run her hands across her body and wished that someone else were there, scorching their fingertips on the feverish heat of her skin. But in that room with that boy, lying still and trying to feel nothing, she was cold as stone.

A nurse came in and checked the chart next to her bed.

'How are you feeling?'

Thirsty,' she croaked.

'I'll get you some water.'

The nurse returned a couple of minutes later with a glass, and helped her sit up and drink. A few minutes after she'd left, Andy arrived. He looked too large for the room, his head almost grazing the ceiling. When he bent to hug her she could smell the cheese Doritos on his breath.

'Don't.' She didn't want to be touched. Her body didn't feel solid enough yet.

'Does it hurt down there?' he asked, releasing her.

'Yes.'

'Oh no, how long will it take to heal?'

'The doctor says anything from a week to six weeks,' she said, and as his eyes widened she realised what he really wanted to know was how long it would be before they could have sex again.

'God, that's a long time. I can't imagine sharing a bed with you every night for six weeks and not being able to, you know,' he said.

'Perhaps you should sleep in the spare room then,' she told him, and watched his face fall. He was so easy to hurt, and it made her feel terrible whenever she did it.

'If that's what you want,' he replied.

'Andy, I'm not trying to exile you. I just want to do this right. Losing my virginity again is something I want to build up to slowly. I want to wait until I'm ready.'

'It's different for boys. I just wanted to lose mine as quickly as possible. And I succeeded. Under a minute, I think it took,' he said, smiling at her hopefully.

She didn't smile back. It wasn't a joke.

*

Andy and Cleo were sitting on the sofa, watching a documentary about the ocean, a blanket over their laps. He was finding it hard to concentrate. Over the past couple of months he'd been as sexually frustrated as a teenager. She'd grown fond of making out with him for what seemed like hours on end, and whilst she actively encouraged him to clamber on top of her for a session of dry-humping, skin-on-skin contact was still strictly prohibited. It was excruciating, but of course he couldn't complain, because that wasn't very supportive. All he could do was sit tight and hope he'd get laid eventually.

He tried to concentrate on the episode they were watching, which was about the epipelagic layer of the ocean, the only part where sunlight penetrated; where luminescent shoals of fish were carried along by the currents and whales glided towards them with open mouths.

'Did you know that whales have hymens too?' he asked Cleo.

She turned to him. 'What are you trying to insinuate?'

'Nothing. Nothing.'

They continued watching. He slung his arm loosely around her and rested his hand lightly on her shoulder. She didn't move, or protest, and he wondered if he should go a step further and try and kiss her. The air in the room suddenly felt very thick.

Cleo stole a glance at Andy. His face was blue from the light of the television screen and he was staring at it in rapt attention; keeping his hands to himself, for once. She wondered what he'd say if he found out that the doctor had given her the go-ahead to resume physical relations a fortnight ago.

She placed her hand lightly on his knee and felt him stiffen at the touch. When she caressed his thigh he shifted in his seat, and as she grazed her fingertips across his crotch she realised the reason for his discomfort. She laid her hand on the bulge and began to massage it gently. After a minute or so, he moved her fingers from his crotch.

'What's wrong?' she asked.

'I just can't cope with any more of this teasing. You keep getting me worked up and shooting me down,' he replied.

She pushed back the duvet and climbed onto his lap, so she was facing him. The hardness of his crotch was making her tingle, and without really thinking about it she began to gyrate against it. A small moan escaped his lips.

'Aren't you enjoying all this? The anticipation?' she asked, as his hands tentatively slid up the back of her t-shirt.

'I feel a bit lost, to be honest. I don't know how to behave around you any more,' he said, looking as if he were about to cry.

A delirious heat flooded her system.

'I'm going to have a quick wash. I suggest that you meet me in the bedroom. I haven't taken the pill recently, so you'll need a condom,' she told him.

His eyes widened. 'Now? We're doing it now?'

'Yes. I'm ready.'

He lay in bed, the covers pulled up to his chin. As the door opened and she entered the room, wearing a white lace nightdress, he began to tremble. What if he ruined it for her the second time round?

She pulled back the covers and slid into bed next to him, and he turned his face to hers.

'Do you want me to go down on you?' she whispered, a couple of minutes later, after they'd fumblingly removed her clothes.

'Sure, of course. If you want to.'

Her mouth had barely touched him when he thought he might

be getting close. He closed his eyes and tried to distance himself by thinking of other things: what to get his mother for her birthday; how to make phytoplankton interesting for his students; why the woman in the flat below had decided to vacuum at eleven o clock at night.

'Andy?'

He looked down. She'd lifted her head and was staring at him with a puzzled expression.

'What's up, babe?' he asked.

'Are you enjoying it? You aren't making any noise.'

'Oh, don't worry; I'm having a lovely time. But I'd like to give you pleasure now.'

'Ok.'

She scrambled up beside him, and he reached for the condoms. It took forever to get through the cellophane wrapping, another age to rip open the condom packet.

'Be gentle,' she whispered.

She felt much tighter than he remembered. Her body, which he'd once known so well, was now uncharted territory. He tried to go as slowly as possible, but even so, the first thrust made her gasp in pain. Over the next few minutes he pushed, stuffed and apologised, until finally their bodies were bumping awkwardly together in the missionary position. Despite their combined ineptitude, he could feel a familiar tightening sensation in his groin.

'Andy... look at me,' she gasped.

He stared into her beautiful green eyes, shuddered, and collapsed on top of her.

'Sorry,' he muttered into her shoulder.

'Why?' she asked.

'You didn't...you know,' he said, rolling onto his back and pulling off the condom.

'That's ok. I'm getting a glass of water. Do you want one?'

'Sure,' he replied, wondering why she didn't want to cuddle.

She stood up and put on her nightdress.

'Did I ruin it?' he asked miserably.

'No. Of course not,' she said, kissing his forehead and standing up. There was a small red stain on the sheets, but she didn't seem to notice.

In the living room the documentary was still playing. On her way back from the kitchen Cleo paused to watch a shoal of fish dart through the clear blue waters. They were coloured such bright yellow it appeared as if they were illuminated from the inside. She envied the way they all headed in the same direction without having to talk about it, their bodies always maintaining equal distance from one another.

She lay down on the sofa and placed her feet on the armrest. Her nightdress fell back, exposing her thighs, and without thinking about it she found her hand sliding between them. Shadows of fish flickered across her body. Under the sea, she would feel weightless. Her entire body would be as wet as the place between her legs. She closed her eyes, and the music swelled to a crescendo. Under the sea there were no words and no memories, just movement; each gesture as soft as dreaming.

Looking For Jim Morrison
– Victoria Hattersley –

He was proving harder to find than she'd imagined.

There had been images of his grave on TV, years ago, when she'd been a child, on an anniversary of his death. The grave had been surrounded by hippies with candles, who'd looked the way she'd pictured her parents in the '60s or '70s. Her mother had always listened to the Doors. She'd watched that film and said it was amazing how alike Jim Morrison and Val Kilmer were. Her mother had said that one day she'd go to Paris and visit the grave too, all by herself, and be free for a while. Then she'd looked around, with a challenge in her eyes.

This graveyard was huge. A city.

For a time she gave up on him. She made a detour to Oscar Wilde, whose tomb was easier to spot because it was a slightly different shade to its neighbours. Most of the others were made of weathered grey stone, but Oscar Wilde's was off-white, and ugly, if truth be told. She stood in front of it and tried to remember what it was supposed to be. There was a male figure that seemed to be flying (something classical, wasn't it?). "His mourners will be outcast men, and outcasts always mourn." True enough.

She wanted to leave him something, as a mark of respect, because he meant more to her than that old dead singer after all. Some people had pinned notes to the tomb but she didn't even have any paper. In the end she pulled out her pouch of tobacco and sprinkled a little around the back. Furtively, in case someone was there to witness such a naked display of sentiment.

But what about Jim Morrison? She hadn't planned to look for him, but now she was here she felt somehow obliged to. She'd thought it would be easy. She'd had this mental image of a procession of musical pilgrims from all over the world, sitting around with guitars and singing and holding hands. You'd be able to hear them from a distance.

It was nothing like that. The place was laid out in silent rows of the dead, lined with oaks and planes and other trees she didn't recognise. And each row spawned others. Sometimes she was sure she'd walked down the same one, twice, or three times. There were ludicrously Gothic mausoleums for distinguished old French families, long forgotten. Some with broken doors so you could walk in and poke around among the cobwebs if you really wanted. They looked as though they should contain plastic skeletons, beckoning, with eyes that illuminated the darkness. She was morbid, she thought, as she left Oscar Wilde behind to continue her search.

Earlier that day Maman the spider had loured over her in the Tuileries Garden. She must have been ten feet high, maybe more. Each leg tapered thinly to the ground, looking too fragile to support her body. Looking up at Maman made her want to curl up in a frightened ball at her feet.

Right in the middle of the sculpture, where her legs met at the top, there was a pouch of some kind, like a weaver's basket. She'd read somewhere that the artist had died recently and that her mother had been a weaver. This artist had lived a long time and done a lot of things in a lot of places. She'd had a Life.

There was a group of kids standing around the spider, laughing.

She thought about how she must look. No make-up on her face. Comfortable shoes, because this was an unfamiliar place and she didn't know how far she'd have to walk. She realised, too late, that it's most important to look your best when you're on your own. Never let yourself down. She looked at her feet and saw she was standing in the shadowy pool cast by Maman's pouch.

It was getting towards late afternoon and there was a slight breeze rustling the leaves overhead. There were other visitors here but nobody made eye contact because they were all doing something slightly shameful, and they knew it. They brazened it out by wearing the same expressions they would if they were in a museum or a park.

She took a detour up some broken steps flanked with tombs on either side, reaching yet another tree-lined path. Up here there was nobody, unless you counted the blackbird – or was it a crow? – sitting on the roof of one of the tombs.

She would have one last try to find Jim Morrison before she had to leave to meet Laura. But yet again there would be nothing to tell; she was tired of being a person with no story of her own.

After a time the path wound its way down again and she found she was almost back where she had started. She reached the place at the top of the wide avenue near the entrance where there was an open circle with a stone monument in the middle. She sat on a bench and tried to make sense of her map. The grave ought to be close by, just a few rows off. But if that was true, how had she not found it before?

She heard the sound of raised voices and looked up to see two people standing a few feet away from her, in front of the monument. It was a man and a woman and they were arguing with no regard for anyone around them. The woman, older than the man, wore a red trouser suit that might once have been expensive but was now rumpled and stained. She had hair almost to her waist, unnaturally blonde and so thin that bits of pink scalp were clearly visible beneath it. The woman's face was creased with anger or something else that she couldn't identify, because she didn't understand the language of it. He was a hunched crew-cut of a man with a torn shirt, and he jittered. Up close, she knew that he would smell of unfiltered cigarettes and spilled beer. That they both would. There was something unsafe about these people. Something unexploded. She got up to walk away.

The couple had fallen silent. The woman put her hand on the man's arm in a gentle, almost supplicating gesture. In answer, he took hold of her head and banged it, hard, against the stone. When she lifted it again there was a livid cut on her forehead. She swayed for a moment and the man stood looking at her as though waiting for a different kind of reaction.

For a moment the stark reality of the act seemed to freeze the three of them together, as though by standing there she had been caught in their radius of violence. But she wasn't taking it in, not really. What came into her mind instead was her mother, and another act of violence, and the dog, all those years ago in Cambridge when she was a child.

And now there was the man with the woman and the bleeding head. How had it not broken into bits with the force of the blow? Heads must be stronger than you think. She found herself moving towards them. She opened her mouth to say something to the man, although she didn't know what it was. But as she stepped forward the woman turned to her, eyes narrowed. She lifted her head and spat in her face.

'Va te faire foutre,' she said.

Now there were other people coming over. A car pulled up and a uniformed security guard heaved himself out. He took hold of the man, who protested, pointing at the woman. Some concerned graveyard tourists tried to look at her bloody head and she promptly burst into tears. Long wails that went on and on.

Wiping the woman's saliva from her face, all she could think was, let her have her head broken then. I'm going to look for Jim Morrison's grave. She gave one last look at the woman who was still crying and clinging on to the man who had tried to break her head. Then she set off in what she hoped was the right direction.

And the dog. It had happened when she had been – eight? She was with her mother that day, shopping for scarves or beads or mirrored cushions or something like that. From shops where everything was expensive but had been made to look as though it wasn't. The dog was on a piece of grass just near the marketplace in Cambridge, off St Mary's Passage. A man was twisting its collar and it was letting out a high-pitched whimpering noise. The man had big black boots and matted dreadlocks. People were protesting but most seemed wary of getting close. His eyes were glittering with something unnatural.

Then the man from the fish stall advanced, fists raised.

'You leave that dog alone or I'll kill you this time. You hear me, I'll kill you.'

The man with the dog turned to face the man from the fish stall. Her mother stepped forward too. She wasn't afraid of anything.

'Is he hurting that dog?' she said. She went right up to the man with the glittering eyes and pointed in his face. 'I'll kill him if you don't,' she said. But she had never really liked dogs. Mother was a cat person.

'Fuck off, all of you,' he shouted. He was teetering on the edge of something, she could tell.

She pulled at her mother's skirts. 'Please Mummy,' she said. 'Please come back.' She heard the whining note in her voice. Her mother looked down but didn't seem to take her in, as though her mind was elsewhere.

Then the police arrived and the dog was taken away in a van. She tugged again at her mother's skirt. At last Mother looked at her properly.

'Why are you frightened of everything?' she said. 'Did you want him to hurt that dog? You can be a very selfish little girl.'

She looked at her feet, fighting back tears because they made Mother angry. It was true: she only cared about herself. No wonder Mother wanted something else.

At this moment she was jolted from her memory by an aging French hippy who had appeared from behind one of the rectangular tombs.

'You are looking for Jim, yes?' he said to her.

'Jim Morrison? Yes, I suppose I am.'

'Come with me, I show you to him.'

He beckoned to her to follow him off the path into the forest of gravestones. She hesitated briefly before obeying.

And there it was; nothing at all. No wonder she hadn't found it. There were no groups of singing flower people holding hands, just this solitary man with a greying mane of hair and a striped waistcoat. He stood over the grave and gestured towards it, with all the pride of a self-appointed guardian.

'C'est Jim,' he said. 'I love him.' He put both hands to his heart.

'Yes, me too,' she said doubtfully. She stood as if to admire the small rectangle of earth and the stone inscribed with the name 'James Douglas Morrison'. No Jim.

'Where is everyone?' she said to the hippy.

'No-one here,' he said. 'Just myself. People used to write notes on it but no more. There was a head, years ago, but somebody took it away.'

'Oh.'

There seemed to be nothing more to say. Then, just as suddenly as he had appeared, the hippy vanished again behind the tomb. When he returned he was leading a man and a woman in shorts, both holding cameras.

'What are we looking at?' said the man in a transatlantic drawl.

'C'est Jim, I love him,' said the hippy.

'Ah, yeah,' said the man, staring at the grave. 'The Lizard King.' They both took pictures.

There was a silence that went on for too long after this, all four of them looking down at the grave. So this is really it, she thought. The place of pilgrimage.

'Well, thank you, I mean merci,' she said finally to the hippy, who ignored her.

The afternoon was fading into early evening and it was really time to go. The good thing, she thought to herself as she walked towards the exit, was that now she had a story to tell Laura. She wouldn't tell her about the fighting couple: it was too awful, and somehow it would be her fault because she hadn't stopped it happening. When people asked her what she had done that day, she'd tell them about the hippy and Jim Morrison. How the world isn't always how you'd imagined it to be.

And she remembered how earlier that day, when she'd stepped out from underneath the shadow of Maman's pouch, the sun had been warm on her back and for a moment she had felt free. Then she thought maybe she understood what it was to be really trapped – and not just by who you were.

'I'm sorry Mother,' she said, leaving the heavy, open gates behind her.

Atacama

– Ann Abineri –

The driest place on earth. 10, 000 feet above sea level. I settle my heavy water container into my shadow. Without water I would die here. I stretch out my shawl and let it drop loosely over my head.

Today I will begin ten yards away from yesterday's starting point. We work alongside one another, spread out across the desert. We have sieves, tools and small sacks. Once Josefina brought a magnifying glass but she laid it down and set her skirt alight. She had to rip the skirt off and beat it, then walk home that night with its tattered hem hanging round her thin ankles.

I start my search by scooping up sand and stones and sieving out the smaller particles. Then I tip the contents of the sieve onto my blanket and pick through this closely. As I work I sort through thoughts that have been sifted many times before.

When Juan was a boy, he played in the gravel near our house. I had to keep telling him not to throw it. Although his throw was weak, I worried about neighbours' property. But he clearly took pleasure in the sounds the stones made as they struck different surfaces. I began to feel that all I ever did was tell him off. Then one day our neighbour Conchita brought over an old tin bucket and showed Juan the noises that could be made when you dropped stones into it. The throwing stopped. For a while.

Our search began over thirty years ago. There were more of us then. Some have given up, worn out, old before their time, eyesight faded. Others have died. At night, if I sleep, I find myself in an endless landscape of stones to sieve and sift. Sometimes I wake excitedly with imagined finds clenched tight in my calloused hands, only to realise it was a dream.

When Juan was fifteen he began throwing stones again. He and other boys would hide in derelict buildings and take it in turns to throw stones at passing soldiers. I did not know this at the time of course. I thought they were playing football or swimming all day. They did those things but they mainly tested out their throw and their nerve on the militia.

We never speak of the monster that did this to our loved ones or the men who carried out his orders. They are beyond any words we can find. We've seen the news reports and sat in the families' balcony at the hearings but we never speak of the men who took our loved ones away. They are still free. When we are in the city, we pass them in the street, going home to their partners and families. We have to ignore them.

I was proud when Juan took up his place at University. He worked hard to support himself there and had little free time but I now know that what time he had was not spent on sport or with a girlfriend but at underground political meetings. These, it turned out, were not secret.

I sort a pile of tiny bone fragments, sometimes smooth, sometimes splintered, and put them into my sack. Occasionally we find teeth. The teeth make me cry, they look so familiar, so recognisable. I don't know whose husband's or son's smile they belonged to but they make me cry.

The evening becomes cool. It can freeze here at night. We should be able to work faster as the temperature goes down but we are tired now. A woman stands, stretches and looks towards the village. One by one we all stand. Exhausted, each of us needing a meal and a night's sleep. I let a last handful of stones trickle through my fingers, unable to overcome the feeling that this handful could be the one.

Back in the village, we tip our sacks into the boxes provided by the forensic pathologist. Once a month he flies in to Calama Airport to look at our finds and select items for DNA matching. The new government has agreed to continue to fund this service until the matter has been settled. What does that mean - settled? What's happened cannot be changed and not only is our search vast, no one knows for sure whether their loved one is here or was dropped, weighted down, over the sea. But there have been finds and so we persist. We have left the rest of our families to come here, to search. They either support us or have moved on.

We live in hope that one day each of us will be able to arrange a burial. In my imagination I see Juan's name on the death certificate, hear the eulogy, and picture the stonemason at work. I promise myself that if this ever happens then I will walk to my son's grave cradling a stone in my pocket, and I will do this every morning until I die. I will build a pile of stones, each small round pebble a thought, a memory or a wish. Then I will be able to close my eyes at night without seeing bones and teeth.

Sacraments

– C.G. Menon –

"Don't call me Granny, Peter. It's *Mummy* today, remember."

Kathleen stood on the platform, Peter's small fingers clutched in her own. A chalked sign overhead swooped and swung on its chain; London, it said, and every clang jarred on – as she put it – her very last nerve. She hadn't been to London since she was six, when she'd been taken to the pantomime at Covent Garden. All she remembered was a howl of applause, coloured lights in the snow, and the cold, sick feeling of needing the lavatory on a packed train platform. She'd made Peter go twice before they left home.

"Those shoes are disgraceful, Nora. He's coming straight out to the shops today."

Nora's little garden was wet and full of sea-breezes, scudding sunlight and the flap and billow of pegged-out laundry. Peter had come running as soon as she'd knocked on the door, and through the kitchen window Kathleen could see Nora dealing briskly with breakfast plates and porridge bowls.

"Gosh, hang on then, love. His coat!"

Nora flung her hands out, the reddened fingers dripping with soapy water. She'd been slim when Davy first brought her home, with a frail, bones-and-eyelashes delicacy Kathleen had tutted over. But Davy had died five years ago, leaving Nora a widow and poor Kathleen just – well, she'd sniffed bravely, just nothing at all. Nora had wrapped herself in fat since then, in ungainly print aprons and spatters of ill-timed tears. It was just like her, Kathleen thought as she trundled out and left the kitchen door wide open, to be so, so – *woolly*.

"That's smashing, I didn't know how I'd stretch to them. Our lad's a little beanstalk!"

She crammed Peter into his coat, tugging and buttoning him with a smacking, jolly sort of relish. Kathleen set her teeth. Nora had a casual way of accepting her offers with something that wasn't quite gratitude, and she resolved that whatever else happened today, she would not be buying Peter shoes. It was his mother's job, after all, to feed and clothe him. She wouldn't want to impose.

Nora waved them down the lane, blowing kisses onto the wind that puffed under their coats and snatched at their ankles. The church was just round the corner, where crocus spears spread a thin green haze. But it would be no use; she knew that already. She couldn't ask Father Adrian. Not even though she'd made her tidy confessions to him for the past ten years; not even though she'd been at every Mass with her hat pinned back and her hassock ready for kneeling. She *had* tried once, after Peter was born.

"To baptise him, Father – you would need the parents' permission?"

Because Davy was dead, she didn't say, and Nora was obstinate with grief and anger – as though it had been *her* son who died – and kept bursting into noisy tears that shook her milk-stained bosom in a most un-widowlike way.

"But, Nora, you *must* have him baptised. It's a sacrament, dear." For Nora had still been dear in those days, if an increasingly intractable dear. Somebody, Kathleen had eventually decided in her squared-off, chopped-down way, had to manage things. But Father Adrian hadn't agreed.

"I'm sorry, Kathleen. But we need to know he'd be raised Catholic, afterwards."

She'd surprised him, Father Adrian explained later over a conscientious supper with the bishop. He hadn't thought she would cry.

By the time they'd been on the train for an hour the clouds had burnt off, and the air was steamed and thick. Peter took his finger out of his mouth and squeaked it over the window pane, chasing a trapped fly.

"It won't know where it is, will it, Granny? When we get to London. It's a *country* fly."

She stared out at the fields, blurring past with their flattened grass and vacant, harmless cows.

"Peter," she began, "after today, Granny will need to make sure you're being brought up correctly. It's a big responsibility." She felt an immense weariness at the thought of what had to be gone through, and fumbled in her handbag to check everything was in place.

His finger continued its damp, dragging squeak, and she sat back with a look of despair. Davy's child, she thought, but surely at five Davy had been brighter, less stolid. A damp wool smell rose from her sleeve and she sniffed at it discreetly. Musty, but she could sponge it. It would see her out.

"Paddington, coming up!" A young guard stuck his head around the door. "Mind the steps, Ma'am, they can be tricky if you're not so steady" – and Kathleen winced.

Her clothes felt bundled and lumpish after the journey, with her cotton blouse tight under the arms. Peter pulled free as she clambered onto the platform, running in circles and shrieking in a high-pitched, excited way that set her teeth on edge.

"Peter – *dear*," she implored, then coughed and began again in a much jollier tone she half-recognised as Nora's. "Let's all calm down."

Her head was beginning to ache, and all around was a sturdy, purposeful bustle. She strode forward, hemmed in by the small spaces of the crowd and checked at every step by Peter's clinging hands.

The sight of a few scruffy plane trees outside lifted her spirits, like seeing a familiar face in a crowd. She didn't dare stop to ask directions, not here in this blackened brick square where cars and people converged with a frightening deliberation. Peter had begun to fidget, and she recognised that bright, ferocious look on his face that always preceded a tantrum. This is my fault, she thought; I am not managing this at all well.

"Don't cry, Peter," she begged, but it made no difference; his mouth squared and he began to howl. "Just think," she coaxed, "after today you'll be baptised. You'll be God's child." And so that was the first sacrament, she thought, held out to her grandson like an extra-special sweetie. Oh, Davy – and a sudden pang shot through her – you should not have died and left me to cope with it all.

It seemed to work, though. Peter snuffled back his tears and a tentative smile began to break through.

"And Mummy won't." He laced his hand into hers.

No, she agreed. Mummy certainly wouldn't.

And then they walked, traipsing hand-in-hand for miles through the endless, eddying streets as Kathleen looked for a church. Her head was splitting and a strange, throat-lumpy sob had lodged beneath her ribs. She started to rest at bus stops, bundling Peter on board whenever one stopped and waiting five or ten tense minutes as the baking streets went by. The Blitz had hit this area badly, and she couldn't quite fix her gaze on anything; people and buildings and the aching gaps in terraces all slid away into a creaking haze. Squinting at a crossroads, she felt a streak of pain so vivid that for a moment she thought one of her hatpins had cut her scalp.

"Granny, there!"

And yes, it *was* there – a crooked church spire wavering in the heat haze above a sloping roof. Peter strained at her hand, his face crunched with the effort of moving her, but she snatched him back. There was something to be done first.

"Peter, you mustn't move an *inch*."

The street had become busy, with a brisk, strutting crowd flowing round them. She shuffled to one side, clumsy with nerves, and undid the clasp of her bag. She'd imagined doing this in private, perhaps in the sanctity of the Ladies' waiting room, but there was no time for that now. It would have to be a public act.

She'd begun it weeks ago, spending hours at the make-up counters while slicked-down lady assistants yawned behind their lacquered nails. She'd marched into the new department store with a month's housekeeping money tucked into her purse and left with a slippery parcel full of stuff that claimed to hide wrinkles, or to take ten years off her age.

She inspected the pots now, crammed in her bag as tight as sparrow's eggs. She hadn't quite dared to ask how each one was used – and there were so *many*, she thought with a collapsing despair. Powder, of course – she recognised that – and lipstick, and a strange oily brush to hide her crow's feet. After each attempt she peered doubtfully in the mirror of her tiny compact, dabbing at her face with hesitant fingertips. Rouge

121

clung to her sagging cheeks, and caked into the seams around her mouth. She'd wiped off the lipstick, which had made her look soiled and wounded instead of the promised ten years younger.

"Mummy," she pronounced finally, turning to Peter with a smeared, hopeful smile. He gaped a little and she gave him a distracted hug, knocking a spill of rouge onto her coat. Straightening up, she opened her bag again and pulled out a plain gold ring with the price tag still attached. She pushed it slowly onto her left hand, and then for a little while – just a little while, she thought, hardly any time at all – some tears streaked down and mixed with her powder.

Climbing the sand-scrubbed steps below that crooked spire, she was expecting somewhere like the village church; a dim space stained with coloured shadows. But instead they walked straight into a bright room, washed with clear sunlight and panelled in wood. The glare hurt her eyes and left her head raw, swollen with her migraine and the make-up and the weight of what was coming next.

A door beside her opened with a flimsy, plasterboard thump, and a man in an unhemmed cassock peered towards them. He seemed very young, with a shaving rash on his neck and reddened spots of eczema at his wristbones. Kathleen's head stabbed with pain as the door banged shut, and she clutched at Davy's hand. Not Davy, she reminded herself – Peter. Peter, of course. She felt with her thumb for the wedding band and rubbed it. At least, she thought, I am respectable, now.

"He's here to be baptised." It was too abrupt, she knew, and she thrust Peter forwards as though to apologise. The priest looked down at him with a smile; a well-used, practised sort of smile, she thought.

"I'm sorry, Mrs – Mrs - ?"

"Mrs Nulty," Kathleen told him.

"But you would need to be a member of this parish. You would need to prepare, you understand."

"I know," she hurried the words out. "But I thought, in an emergency?" She pushed a hank of hair from her face and gave him a stricken smile.

He hesitated, scratched at the side of his wrist. "Are you his... might I ask what the relationship is?"

Kathleen swallowed. That throat-lumpy sob had grown, was bubbling into a quick and gasping breath that didn't suit this scrubbed church at all. At her side Peter had begun to sniffle.

Davy had cried too when she'd carried him to the village church. It had been a desolate, grown-up sort of sobbing, that she hadn't heard from him before. Father James had listened to her, had stammered – *without the sanctity of marriage* – he'd said, then coughed and cast about for words. Eventually he'd lifted Davy from her arms and turned to her mother instead; Mrs Nulty grim and iron-haired as she agreed to bring David Nulty up in the sight of God. Kathleen had huddled in a pew and her milk had started to come, seeping out on her pink silk bodice while Davy cried in his grandmother's arms. Later that night she'd sponged and sponged but the stain, it turned out, was there for good.

"Mummy!" Peter howled and she looked down at him in the clear, white light. Quite an ugly child, she thought, trussed up in his coat like that. Davy had been beautiful.

She brushed at her coat, smudging the rouge into a reddened splotch. It wouldn't see her out after all, the coat was quite ruined and she turned to walk with sedate, small steps down the aisle as the priest stuttered something she didn't quite hear. She closed the door after her, shutting all that glare politely away. Then down the steps, and Peter clinging as they tramped past streets and bombsites where twisting white bindweed grew. And then suddenly nothing, only a cloud of birds in the beating sky and Nelson's Column stretched up like taffy.

"Lions!" Peter squalled when he saw the statues, and dragged her towards the fountain. She leant against its rim, watching him drench his feet in their too-small shoes, and scooped up a palmful of water to swab at the stain on her coat. It trickled down over her wedding ring and dripped into the silky parting of his hair. "Granny?" he asked in surprise, and she shook her head and put her finger to her lips.

"I baptise thee, Davy," she began, and drew him onto her lap, scrubbing with wet hands at a coat that had seen much better days.

Folding

– Patricia Mullin –

The small boxes arrived one at a time and regularly. Often reconstructed from older packaging with product names in foreign scripts that formed curiously angled geometric patterns. My flat was on the ground floor and I studied at a desk in the bay window where daily I watched the postman making his way up the street, by the time he reached the Greek Cypriot household two doors away he was often holding a box and the letters in his hand. At this point I got up from my desk and went to the door. The boxes were always for Adam, who lived on the third floor. Sometimes, Adam would race downstairs, taking the steps two at a time and arriving breathless beside me at the front door. He would thank us both, never quite meeting our eyes and immediately run back up the stairs as energetically as he had descended.

On the days when Adam was out I carried the box upstairs and left it on the floor outside his door. I was curious because they were weightless and they came from far off countries, often East Asia. I rarely encountered Adam long enough to make enquiries about these little boxes or their contents, he was either in a hurry or locked away upstairs; he wasn't a talker. Occasionally we would collide in the hallway, me coming in, Adam going out and we would dance awkwardly in the narrow passageway, lifting our arms out of the way and skirting around one another in the British manner in order to minimise the possibility of physical contact.

One morning as the postman handed me a tiny box my telephone rang, distracting me, and without thinking I took the box into my room and set it down on my desk. It sat there all morning; periodically I would break from my dissertation and pick the box up. It was light as a feather and the stamps confirmed it originated from Japan. I went back to my work. Later, I turned it over and tried to peer into a crevice, but the expert nature of the packaging left no gap. I don't know at what point I decided to open it, but once the thought had lodged in my mind I found I couldn't retreat from the idea.

I gave more thought to opening this box than to my politics dissertation. I considered denting or crushing part of the box exposing the contents, I could say that it had arrived damaged. In the end I decided to lift some of the packing tape and then take a small knife and cut neatly through a seam in the box, lifting the side away. I had an idea that interfering with other people's mail was illegal, but that didn't bother me too much, after all, no one would ever know.

I took the box to the kitchen, wanting to see what was inside this box was a compulsion that I couldn't fight. I drew the knife through the tape and lifting the opening I peered into the interior. It was filled with soft shredded paper, like the soft bedding used for pet mice, I pulled some of it out onto the work surface. Antennae quivered — I emitted a shriek. Never good with creepy crawlies, I backed away and from a safe distance I waited for the insect to move and wondered where the kitchen tongs were. I eyed my tormentor, who remained motionless. Then the logical part of my brain clicked in and I began to doubt that it was alive — of course it wouldn't have survived the journey and it would have had to clear customs; there are strict rules about importing exotic creatures. Gingerly, I sidled up to the kitchen drawer that contained the tongs and grabbing a deep saucepan, in one swift, nervy move I propelled the insect into the bottom of the pan and slammed on the glass lid. Pressed against the wall I waited for a buzzing, ticking or flapping, waited for sounds of life, distress, or escape attempts. Nothing. Finally, I concluded that it was dead. Bolder now, I removed the lid and nudged the creature with the tongs. Peering closely I laughed, mainly with relief. It was constructed from paper. Picking it up, I turned it over; it was a perfectly rendered beetle, pre–historic looking and remarkably realistic. I made myself a coffee, relaxed and went to look it up on the Internet. It was a Trilobite with an armoured shell; found in Southeast Asia and India they live on land and come in many weird and wonderful, if scary, forms. This was enough distraction from my dissertation for one day, so I re–packed the paper beetle into its box and placed it outside Adam's door.

That should have been the end of it. But over the next couple of weeks I opened two more packages. The first was a flying Atlas Beetle, again small and formed in paper. Then an altogether larger box arrived; it said *open this way up*, so I did. It was startling, it was a Cobra — part coiled and posed with its jaw stretched open and ready to strike. I packed it away very quickly and once again left it outside Adam's door.

Feeling guilty I avoided Adam, making sure I moved away from the window when he went out and slipping inside my flat as soon as I heard him on the stairs. Then one day I found a package outside my door. It was a tiny cardboard box. I picked it up and took it to my desk and sat staring at it for a long time. Adam knew, I had not fooled him. I wondered if he was angry. Carefully I lifted the lid, it was an acorn, a perfect little green acorn and there was a label it read *From little acorns…* I smiled, it was a friendly gesture. A week later he left another box for me, it was an origami bowl of stunning complexity and then a few days later a ghostly Nautilus arrived with a note asking me out to dinner. I returned a note accepting the invitation.

I was enjoying this origami courtship and gave more thought about my appearance than usual. When he tapped on my door I found I was quite nervous. We were two people who had shared the same front door for two years yet self–conscious in one another's company. Adam asked only if I liked fish and kept the destination a secret. We took the Victoria line; the restaurant was Japanese, the fish raw.

Adam ordered for us, a succession of small bowls and plates arrived and I relaxed. The food was fresh, healthy, and the fish tasted good. I apologised for opening his mail, I said that I didn't know what had come over me, explaining that this was the first criminal act I had ever committed and that I was otherwise a worthy citizen. He laughed and then asked what I thought of the origami creatures. I said they were amazing and with that he was off, talking passionately; telling me how he started paper folding as a child using the instructions on the back of an annual. Adam explained that origami aficionados came from all over the world and that historically, in Japan, sacred offerings and rituals warded off evil spirits; paper attracted good spirits. Origami, he said, was used in Shinto weddings and Samurai warriors exchanged good luck paper tokens. These days American physicists were involved, developing equations to describe the physics of curved–crease structures because, he explained, origami transforms the flimsy into a strong flexible three dimensional object and is used in the design of airbags and satellites. A publisher had commissioned him to write a book for industrial and technology designers; the modern–day applications for origami were, according to Adam, legion.

All the time Adam was talking, I was looking at him; he was far more attractive than I had previously noticed. His hair was a bit long and shaggy, his uniform was dull, jeans and a sweater, but he had kind brown eyes, and he bore a passing resemblance to a skinny folk singer my mum had liked. When we got to the front door, he asked if I would like to come up for coffee and look at his origami, I made a corny joke about his 'etchings' but he didn't get the reference. Later, after we'd slept together, I explained it to him and he laughed, embarrassed, that wasn't his intention he protested, no I thought, but it was mine. We fell into a pattern of eating together and folding in the evenings, then enjoying sex. For a bit of geek Adam was skilful in bed. He left packages outside my door, an origami vase and flowers, a lampshade and later, a dress.

Distracted by Adam, I was struggling with my postgraduate studies and my tutor expressed her concern, I was falling behind and some of the research was proving hard to source and, when found, was contradictory. Adam told me that folding would relax me; he said it was a meditative ritual. The Internet was the source of images of extraordinary paper structures and mesmerised by the forms I watched as Adam's hands deftly folded and turned the paper with speed and precision. I gave in to this compulsion, folding daily, I lost the impulse to write and I missed tutorials and a meeting with my supervisor.

My mother visited, took one look at the state of my flat and told me to pull myself together. I said it was the dissertation — that I was working on it day and night. Later I realised she had a point; I hadn't come this far to fall at the last hurdle. I told Adam folding would have to be curtailed; I needed a break from 'us'. I told him not to take it personally. He looked stricken, he didn't understand. I tried hard to concentrate, but the Second World War was a long time ago and my enthusiasm for the Kellogg-Briand Pact of 1928 and its success or failure waned. Wars were bloody and interesting; treaties were their dull consequence and were inevitably broken.

It became awkward when Adam and I met at the front door, I found myself avoiding his gaze. He bombarded me with notes, loving, hurt, then menacing; his obsession had transferred to me. I moved my desk into an alcove away from the bay window and I stopped collecting the post.

Then one morning I found a box outside my door, I opened it. It contained a perfect origami heart and a small craft scalpel. There were a set of dotted lines on the heart, indicating where to cut. I looked at the heart, but put it aside. I tried to write but it was hopeless, the heart troubled me. I lifted the scalpel and pierced the heart drawing the blade carefully along the cut line as a surgeon might, recoiling when a red liquid squirted onto my face and shirt. A note sprung up *You have broken my heart*, I pushed the box away from me standing up so suddenly that my chair fell clattering onto the floorboards. There was a pungent smell, I dipped my finger into the red liquid and lifted it to my nose. I recoiled, it was blood. Animal blood, human blood? Somehow I knew it was his.

Gradually, I retreated to my bedroom, I closed the bay window curtains and I arranged to have my shopping delivered and tried to work. I thought about leaving, but I had become inert. I heard Adam telling the postman I was out — now he was keeping my post. The University emailed me, I hit delete without reading them. Then my mother emailed, the University had sent a letter to my home address, I must attend a board. She complained that she hadn't heard from me in weeks, why didn't I answer the phone, was I alright? I told her lies, reasoning that she wouldn't identify with the fear that a paper heart and some plaintive notes could induce. I slept through days, didn't wash and stayed in my filthy clothes. I listened for every creak and muffled sound and I heard the rhythm of his breathing on the other side of my door. One night I looked out of my window and marvelled at the crescent of a new moon suspended freely in space, then Adam's shadow cast itself on the yard below. Another note arrived *This will be the last box.* I waited until the house was silent and opened the door a crack, I snatched the box and secured the door. I took it back to bed with me and lay there. It was hours before I found the courage to open it. Trembling, I lifted the lid. It contained a pair of origami hands, palms upward, wrists displayed and another scalpel. Across each wrist there was a broken line directing me where to cut.

Leda's Swan

– Margaret Meyer –

On that first night, the heat – so hot, so late – was scorching, or maybe it was the heat between them. She would always remember that. She was out of her depth and a bit drunk on the electric adventure that was Zee. In a recess of the club she pinned him to her; currents pulsed through them both. They left the bar and drove to hers where he unzipped them, expertly and without delay. Dark lay thickly over them, a quilt into which he sank little calls and cries. He was irrepressible, stiff and ready to go again just an hour later, labouring so tirelessly through the night that everything below her pelvis felt damaged. Laughing, he helped her up. They had both to go to work. They soaped each other under the thin spray of the shower. Water was her element, was a relief. Good humouredly she fought him off again.

All day she went back and forth from the aviary to the washroom, partly to keep wet, but also for the remnants of his scent. In the narrow mirror she caught herself smiling. They'd fixed to meet again on Thursday. But at 5.05 his car, conspicuously American, drew up. He was two days early and checking himself in the rear-view mirror. He wasn't really her type, a look of Elvis about him, doughy and indolent. On the other hand it was really something: an entry-level water nymph like her, being courted by a god so exalted. She liked the excuse to leave early, was part-way through gathering up her papers, when Zee came in with his searing smile. Everything capitulated. It made quite a statement, leaving like that, with his arm proprietorially around her waist – and somehow easier to dismiss his glances at the more comely students.

Outside in the blaring heat. 'Are you thirsty?' he asked, reaching for her. She was parched, though not for drink. 'Not really,' she said. His touch was pure voltage, but she stopped him. 'Not here.' A smile unspooled across his face. 'Leda,' he said. 'Where'd you get a name like that?' They drove to his where he insisted on pouring Green Russians. The colour, the smell of them took her all the way back, to college and optimism. While she sipped, his thick hands were already at work, unfastening. Her breasts made him frantic. When finally she returned to the Green Russian all the ice had melted. He brought more from the freezer, tipped some into her drink and some down her back. It was a game, but she nearly brained herself on the corner of the coffee table. 'So sorry,' he said, and went on saying it, ladling the rest of the ice into a makeshift compress. His voice had a crust of something, wit or derision, she thought she could hear. He took her home, they kissed for a long time on the porch under a sprawling Mediterranean sky. She let him in for a nightcap. He was still there ten months later, with scarcely a virgin surface in the house.

She knew exactly what he was, but thought she could temper it. He was adept at bending the truth, or bending in the face of truth, and after a while everything got so pliable, she herself was bent out of shape. In the mornings mist brewed in the crucible of the valley, before rising to be burnt away; mornings when she knew she had drifted too far into Zee's embrace. His leaving in a rush of sex and endearments. *Thinking of you every hour, every day. Z.* he messaged, from somewhere far-flung. She liked to stand by the bedroom window, studying the vapour trails of other pilots' jets. That was where his signal was strongest. She wondered where her life was going, the trajectory of *them*, what else could she message back? They had their own world in which everything was gradually bifurcating. For instance: Zee was here; Zee was not here. Long haul, short leave and he was home, jetlagged and stubbly and ashen. Then gone again. *Can't wait to come – back! Can't wait to undress – you!* His prick was indefatigable, he liked her to free it from the hair that feathered into his crotch. When he was home he would hold her, all day and all night, but in the bedside cabinet at his place there was a stash of pictures, all of them females, some of them mortal. She recognised at once the lie of his arm over women, over shoulders more smooth-skinned or yielding than hers. There was another picture too, of a pair of children with Zee's prominent nose and long neck, the same intent eyes with the little flaming pupils.

Once their novelty had gone she was afraid he'd find her empty. 'Never to me,' he said, gallantly. He went on one knee. He was in it for the long haul; the too-many lay-overs with too-many women he wanted to bring to a close. 'We can mate for life, or we can fall apart,' Zee said, convincing even himself. He would burn all the photographs, even the one of the children, and so he did, turning it to ash in his hand.

He hadn't wanted her to work but she continued anyway, winning another grant, this one for researching the breeding habits of migratory seabirds. It turned out that her voice was perfect for the podium, could smooth out the coarse facts of endangerment or extinction. She was charming with sponsors, finding comfort in their bars, and enthused without prompting about the local aperitif because she sampled it herself most nights. Zee came home for their first few anniversaries. On their fourth, roses came instead and he called from Jakarta, or was it Singapore? On their fifth, he texted: *Delayed.* Ash from Iceland was fouling the airways Zee favoured, and would fall again he said, when at last he called her; tomorrow and tomorrow and days after that. Of course there was weather, there was always weather; every marriage encountered storm fronts. She felt something give, could feel trust haemorrhaging through a rent in the fabric of *them*, because Zee was quite capable of making fair weather if he chose.

In the café her friend offered to take her phone away for the evening. He refilled her glass and lifted his chin in a movement that said, behind you, and as she twisted around there was a leaping second of hope that Zee might be home after all.

The young woman, more beautiful than Leda perhaps, stepped forward. She wanted to say something about Zee. What had Zee been thinking? To have given their address? The bar doors were open; Leda couldn't quite hear what the girl was saying over the tide of noise from the street, or maybe it was inside Leda's head. It turned out that Zee had not disclosed the address. Zee had been careless, and she had followed his trail here. The girl's lips kept moving. Leda looked, and saw that they were bitten. The young woman gestured to show that Zee had bitten them. Through her injured mouth the girl spewed words until she choked and looked away. Just for Leda the girl opened her leather jacket. Her skin was red and blistered. She was seared all the way down. The fact of what Zee had done suddenly gelled and set around Leda like concrete. Quietly, the girl started to sob. She was a raped girl. Glances clung to her as she left.

Of course he wasn't capable of anything static. Zee was an alternating current impossible to earth. He was a lightning strike. He was amps. He was wattage. He was the god of surprises, of ambuscade.

All the way home she fought herself, tears, rage. Now she must make sense of the fibres she'd found on his uniform, the brown gold silver of the hair palette. She let herself into their apartment and immediately felt its barrenness. She took a drink out to the terrace and sipped it, thinking about the children; the ones in the picture, the ones who would not, now, be.

Into the evening silence a thought inserted itself. She closed her eyes and saw what life would be like, rinsed of the presence of Zee. She had never contemplated it. She had made no preparations. When she opened her eyes the thought was still there, grit in the oyster, and the phone was ringing.

It was Circe, friend and one-time colleague, a botanist on an island populated mainly by men. Circe had been at the wedding, steeling herself to wish them well. Once a year she called. Leda understood that the call was an inquiry; over the years they had tactfully skirted the truth of Zee and the photographs and his many absences. Now it was suddenly possible to admit the facts.

The marriage, said Leda, was pushing her to the edge.

'What edge?' queried Circe.

To the edges of islands, cliffs, because tonight all the ground had been cut clean away.

'But you've always known,' said Circe.

'Known?'

'That he cheats.'

'I guess,' said Leda. Weariness rested on her.

Circe laughed. 'The guy is a pig. I told you.' This now was irrefutable; there were lips and other bitten things to prove it. 'Come over,' said Circe, into the silence. 'Put it on his tab. There are plenty of guys over here, I can introduce you.'

Leda went to the edge of the terrace, considering. In the beginning, in the spate of them, Zee had told her his true name, the one he had to obey. So then she called, summoning him. Above her head, a comet incinerated itself across a livid sky.

On the way to the airport in Zee's car and the heat beginning to lift from the day. On the seat beside her lay his wilted penis, wrapped in wax paper, a small parcel of charcuterie. She hadn't really meant to, had meant only a gesture, but the blade's sharpness had ambushed them both. As she left she'd seen the flame-shaped nub of his new member already sprouting, but there remained the problem of his theatrical sobbing, which she could still hear. She put the roof down, willing the wind to excise the sound of it.

She drove along the coast road, Nice, Antibes and Cagnes, flicking by like a newsfeed. She was tiring now. Where the coast grew rocky and she knew there were caves, she stopped, parking as close as she could to the shore. She went unsteadily beachwards, dropping her phone as she went. The tide was low and she had to walk a long way out, until she felt salt water licking her thighs. She unwrapped the sticky paper. The cock rolled from it and hung suspended in the clear water. Below it she could see slow creatures – coral, molluscs, the red scar of a sea slug sprawled on the seabed – all going on with their lives. The prick was fizzing like aspirin, starting to boil the surface, and when she bent her head to the waterline she could hear, oh, all the frequencies, long wave, short wave, though she wasn't sure whether it was the sea talking. She took a step back. Muscular waves were rolling in, pushing and moulding. The prick was all gone and foam was piling up. In it there was a shape with the buds of arms and legs, readying itself.

She hadn't considered a birth. But of course there were plenty of precedents, other nymphs and goddesses made from clotted water. She let herself slide. The sea wrapped itself around her. Silence welled in her like a rising tide. Relief grew over her skin like scales. She was under, folded into her proper place and the source of herself, and of the foam child if it was coming. She lay full stretch in the rocking water while darkness washed down the evening sky. There was time, she thought, to catch the child and hide it, before she herself was caught.

Colin

– Julie Kemmy –

Colin was a bit of a rogue; I had known that ever since the early days when he'd tried to sell me his clapped-out v-dub that he'd admitted with no shame had no heater and that there was a 'special' way you had to tease the gear stick into place. But somehow we got along because everything felt so easy and good-natured. He did a lot of handyman work for me, on and off that whole summer. We became sort-of friends; he always made me smile. He made things seem laid-back and as though convention was a ridiculous thing. Life seemed full of possibilities in his company, and it gave me real pleasure that he liked spending time with me. That's a dangerous sensation for a woman of a certain age, vulnerable to the slightest bit of interest.

I wanted to ignore the attraction because he was, after all, half my age. He wasn't gorgeous; he was quite odd-looking, with a slightly pudgy dough face that seemed to have no angles at all, but his body was alright – not muscle-bound, not skinny, but lean enough; this was what I was happy to imagine, anyway. He made me think about it; I mean he didn't exactly ask me to, but it was inevitable that I did, in the quiet disgrace of my private thoughts. I would try to be firm with myself, but the attraction was so strong that I'd find myself aware of him somewhere in the periphery of my consciousness, and I would give myself the necessary talking-to. The fact is, though, he intruded on a daily basis.

I was starting to get nervous in his presence, in case I gave myself away. I didn't want to be humiliated; obviously he wouldn't want me. Why would someone in their early 30's want someone with such noticeable lines and droop? Not to mention the lack of comparable vitality. He was a dynamo compared to me. He was a lazy worker sometimes, taking his time at my expense, but he was always chatty and engaging and vibrant. I felt so dull and boring in comparison.

Tuesday he came round again. I wanted him to fix the picture-rail and the holes in the wooden floor in my study. We talked about materials and how long it would take, and I could feel the heat as he stood next to me. I felt so guilty that I was having these thoughts about him, and was sure he would be able to read my mind. My cheeks started burning, and my smile became more and more fixed while my thoughts became chaotic; I hoped desperately that he wouldn't notice.

I should have moved away, but it was completely magnetic.

He was teasing me. "What have you done to your hair today – that looks nice," he said, and reached to touch my head, patting a curl.

It wasn't a sexy or seductive touch; it was matter-of-fact and quick. All the same I practically jumped, flustered, alarmed, distressed and embarrassed all in one. He could have been a cat, playing with a panicked mouse. I looked at the floor; then quickly I picked up the colour charts from my desk, my hands shaking slightly. "Will you be able to do the painting as well?" I asked, looking fixedly at the charts since I was unable to look into his eyes.

He stood even closer, brushing his arm against mine as he bent to look down at the chart too. "Have you decided what colour yet?"

"Er, no," I had to admit.

"Well I can fit something in, soon as you make your mind up."

I could hear the smile in his words. It made me slightly annoyed, which I guess was how I psychologically groped my way back to a sense of control, so I wasn't quite prepared for the arm that came around my shoulders, or the gentleness of his touch. I felt so overcome I just stood there, every visible part of my skin reddening like a stain was being painted on me, travelling slowly from my chest to my hairline. I was frozen to the spot, trying to get my eyes to focus on the colour charts.

"Maybe you need a little help?" He was definitely pressing against me. And on the word 'help', his hand gave a little emphatic squeeze to my shoulder.

I jarred myself into action, shrugging his arm off. "What are you doing?"

"Keep your shirt on, I was just being friendly. I thought you might like it…"

"Like what?"

"A little bit of…you know…." Again, the smile. Lopsided, teasing. "No worries, we just get on, don't we?"

He put his arm around me again, and this time I didn't jump away, but I couldn't feel comfortable with it either. Somewhere in my lower belly I felt a sensation of something falling. "This is wrong; you're so young…" I said, struggling to make sense of what was going on. "You don't mean this. You're just out to humiliate me." I could hear myself sounding petulant.

He put his hands up in a gesture of giving in, and moved slightly back from me. "Whatever you say…let's just be friends, hey? Don't want to spoil that. I wasn't bothered about the age thing, but you know best, I'm not gonna make you feel bad." Again, he touched my hair. He could sense my upset dissipating and moved closer, putting his arms around me in a bear hug. "Nothing inappropriate, alright?" I nodded and looked up at him. Bastard moved in for a kiss so quickly I didn't have time to deflect his movement and he was so sudden but gentle in his pressure on my lips, and then he broke away from me again; I almost fell backwards into the desk when he let me go.

"No, nothing inappropriate," I agreed. I tried to feel calm. He knew what he had done. He looked pleased with himself. My emotions were jangled, clumsily raw. How did I find this so easy when I was young? He could have ruined it all with that kiss, by doing the usual cliché of passion and trying to stick his tongue down my throat – the very fact that it was so chaste and loving made me want him more than ever.

I knew I wouldn't follow this through. I was a coward and knew I would rather die than let him see and experience my physical self. I didn't want him to have that power over me; I figured it would be a very short time before I was pathetically in need of him, and it definitely wouldn't take long before the novelty would wear off for him. It was lose/lose. I had a sneaking suspicion (or was it paranoia?) that he was just taking the piss anyway. He probably laughed with his mates about me behind my back.

The kiss was something else though. I couldn't get it out of my head. He left that day knowing he had me hooked.

The following Monday I made an effort to be out when he came round to do the painting; I left the key for him under a pot and invented errands and saw friends I hadn't been in touch with for ages. I came home to a note saying he would be finished the next day and could I leave a cheque. Shit. I thought I had plenty of time to work up some defences, or at least invite someone round and then in safety say hello and chat for a few minutes. Instead I had to face him alone: there was no way my pride would allow me to avoid him altogether.

I stayed upstairs out of his way for half the morning, and then crept down. He didn't appear to notice me at all, so I went to the kitchen and started making a mug of tea for him. He was on a small step-ladder, painting gloss on the new picture-rail. The room looked lovely – fresh and ready for my new life working from home. When he saw me in the doorway, he stepped down and held out his hand. I stared at it stupidly, then realised he was reaching for his mug. "Cheers," he said, raising his arm as he took the mug from me, and then lifted it straight up to drink. "What d'you think?" he said, casting his eyes around the room and noisily slurping at his tea. He looked at me as he drank, waiting for a response.

"You've done a great job, as usual," I said. "Much quicker than I expected, too."

"Ah well, that's 'cause you've been avoiding me, so I've had no-one to distract me." He smiled, as though this was a joke. There was a pause, but he carried on staring at me. "Look, I'm sorry if I upset you. No hard feelings, eh?"

"You haven't upset me Colin; I've just been really busy. In fact, I've got to go out again in a minute, so I'll just write out your cheque and get going." I made a show of looking through my bag.

"Oh, like that is it," he said, nodding.

"What? *What?*" I wasn't going to play this game.

"You're being pissy with me because I kissed you."

At the word 'kiss', the heat travelled up my face again. I couldn't look at him.

"Jeez! Don't take it all so seriously. I'll be out of your hair in no time." He pretended to be huffy, but it didn't feel true. To be honest, I don't think he cared either way. He was a chancer.

"I'm not afraid of you," I said, certain only that this would make things worse but unable to stop.

"Could've fooled me. But it's fine, you go meet your friends or whatever it is you've got to do. I'll make everything tidy and get going before you get back." He handed me the mug, and started up the ladder again.

"I'm not going to snog you just to convince you." I was very aware of the difference between the words snog and kiss. "It wouldn't feel right, so there just isn't any point."

"Point? Why does there have to be a point?" He stopped, brush in mid-air. "I just want to live. No harm in that, is there?" He turned back to finish the edge of the picture rail and I noticed that his hands were perfectly steady, and his concentration was focussed entirely on the line.

"I can't just be in the moment; there's tomorrow you know, and everything means something. You learn these things when you get older." I sounded pompous even to myself.

"Maybe, maybe not," he said, stepping down from the ladder for the last time and placing the paintbrush carefully in the jar on the floor. "Doesn't keep you warm at night though, does it?" He was doing the cheeky grin again, and moved towards me. "All I need to do is slip my hand down inside your knickers and you'd soon learn to be in the moment, believe me." His voice was low and intense. He stood right in front of me, his face right next to mine, but he was careful not to touch me. My fear was laughable, but I'd caught something sickening and threatening in the way he'd said it. I visualised him doing it (as he knew I would) and my heart raced. When I didn't move, he hesitated for just a couple of seconds and then turned from me. My belly was dancing flip-flops.

152

I started writing out his cheque, trying hard to keep my hand steady. He busied himself with taking his dust-sheet and ladder out and putting them by the front door. He put his head round the door to the study, a picture of innocence as he took the cheque. "I should have charged an extra few quid on top, for the wet dreams…" he said, and took his tools out to his van.

I'm Not Christiane

– Nicola Miller –

She wanted to be Christiane F without the johns, baby prostitutes and the hand jobs behind Zoo station in seventies Berlin.

She copied the skinny trailing neck scarf of the actress who played Christiane in the eponymous film and pulled on faded drainpipe jeans fastened with an old leather bootlace, woven through home-punched holes in the denim zip-flap. Shod in heeled spike boots in suede so old it had developed worn shiny patches, she wore a shrunken denim jacket, her hair loosely brushed and badly dyed, falling in hanks, over shoulders and face. Eyes were soot rimmed in cheap Tu Kohl bought from Woolworths and sometimes applied in the local park using the stainless-steel surface of the park slide as mirror, one hand holding back her hair.

Her walk was loping, at times stalking: she fancied her walk as a prowl but it took some work, and her length of limb was afforded by the heels and not from superior genes. Her louche attitude was not genetically acquired or something that came to her by privileged birth and landed family, so, despite her nascent drug addiction and extreme youth, there would be no chance for her of being whisked away in a sleek car to a rehab somewhere isolated - Cape Town, Arizona or even the Priory. Her options were limited which over-inflated her sense of pride.

The drugs? They were part of what kept her special, protected from the mundane and the suburban by her veil of numbed indifference and pupils constricted against the harsh light of outside. The track marks she was proud of but kept hidden although they provided her with a map of her progress and acceptance into a group of people she had admired and craved approval of from afar, for so long. Her raggle-taggle band of friends became a dysfunctional replacement for a family who were even worse.

Now she is in her early-middle years and clinging onto that memory of herself as she stands in front of a limed-oak mirror in a shop piled high with fake-wolf fur throws, hand-thrown mugs in cloudy, smudged glazes and baskets full of expensive trinkets that clink and rustle as she runs her fingers through them. A middle class, thick-round-the-middle matron is reflected painfully back at her, both hands frozen like those of a thief caught in the act of dipping into a pocket. The thought "I AM NOT THIS PERSON" wrenches and pummels away; she is affronted by her life as it appears, reflected by the mirror.

Her mind's eye is a zoetrope of images from the past, many of them chaotic and sliding into each other like a cinema verite. She once read a cheap Sidney Sheldon potboiler on a long plane journey about jewel and art thieves. In this glamorous world, black-clad cat burglars slipped into museums and private houses, flitting between Gstaad, The Prado, in Madrid and the South of France. They attended parties where expensively coiffed and scented women slinked, Cartier panther bracelets coiled around their delicate bone-pale wrists as they drank champagne cocktails beneath Goya's ornately framed Black Paintings. The thieves watched and waited and noted. As their targets retired for the night, they passed noiselessly through windows and curled their bodies around infra-red security beams in order to reach safes and securely protected bibelots then performed complicated mathematics and physics with alarms, keypads and dials.

Her former exploits in contrast, which included a raid upon a chemist in a small country town, were rather less glamorous. No cat's cradle of red beams awaited her gang of semi-stoned reprobates – just a darkened barred door to conquer and a small formica-fronted DDU cupboard bolted to a wall within. The cupboard contained the town's weekly supply of morphine and sleeping tablets for the pain ridden and insomniac. Instead of stealthy robber silence and the distant gaiety of party music and laughter, her soundtrack was the crisp snap of bolt cutters, harsh stertorous breathing and glass crunching underfoot as she stood by the getaway car and watched her blue-lit accomplices enter the shop. A jangling alarm rang out as though announcing the end of a fairground ride, startling her. She cringed as the shadowy figures inside the store wiped out both the florescent tubing and security light above the cupboard with a single hammer blow and tore it away from the particle board wall. Then, half dragging and carrying the cupboard, her accomplices burst out of the back door, throwing themselves and their spoils into the waiting car and she sprawled, half sitting, half crouching, on the back seat, a barely adequate look-out as the car sped off.

The torn cupboard spewed its guts into the foot well: giant bottles of viridian physeptone syrup not yet diluted; glass ampoules of morphine snugly clipped into their plastic trays; fat tubs of Valium and the prized 'eggs' - slippery gelatine orange capsules packed with a sleeping draught. They had also managed to boost several blister packs of 'Jacks', a morphine-based pill which produced a peculiar rush upon injection - an itchy cramping across the palms of the hands - craved by some, hated by many but those who loved it were willing to pay a good price. Sitting in the back seat and unbeknown to the two men upfront, she slipped a few blister packs down the side of her boot for later, insurance against the inevitable horse trading which is the trademark of the backsliding user/dealer. Jacked up on little more than adrenalin and the security of knowing there'd be no need to score for weeks, the car embarked upon a 2 a.m. drive across the county border. The idea was to bury most of their stash on some farmland for a couple of days until the fuss died down and the local drugs squad had tired of questioning uncooperative junkies who tenaciously clung to the mantra 'do not grass'.

Sugar-beet fields in the heat of a late summer night are dizzyingly synaesthesic, pitch dark except for shadows cast by a low Norfolk moon and the splotched stars in their bowl of sky, creamily white. Loot in hand, they stumbled and dug through layers of decaying leaves, partially digested by slugs, occasionally stepping onto the bulbous roots pushed out of the ground by weeks of unusually warm days and nights. The roots popped underneath her spiked boots with, she believed, a discernible hiss, releasing their sugary vegetal reek and her stomach, delicate on its opiate-tender diet of cottage cheese and orange ice lollies, roiled.

Rural folk have turned a blind eye to goings-on in fields since time began although she failed to fully appreciate this. Bickering between them flared up - a nasty snarling coiled thing that had been tensed to strike for hours, intermittently quelled by an occasional passing headlight which illuminated the field, turning them into bizarre frozen scarecrows as they attempted to hide in plain sight. Every pair of headlights threatened to belong to the Thames Valley drug squad who were the eighties junkie version of the Candy Man and believed to be everywhere after the rumour went round that they were on secondment to the county police. Arguments broke out again: the depth of hole, how to mark it for a return, why hasn't anyone bought plastic to cover the sodding thing, where the FUCK are we?

Decades later in the town she lives in, the autumn sugar beet campaign is under way again and a burned-toffee fetor cloaks the town. Leaving the shop, whose expensive Feu-de-Bois Diptyque candles only add to the funk in the air, she pulls her thin woollen muffler close to her mouth. The smell still penetrates but her response to it is masked: like a poker player she has become habituated to hiding her reactions from others and where the heroin once accomplished this, she now has only herself and her scarf which she still treats as some magical apotropaic thing.

Back then, thinner and more brittle, she favoured the *Cravate Fluide* style of scarf which, like Christianne, she used as a tie for her arm. At that point, life did not easily accommodate baggage of any kind and so she travelled light, choosing trammels which were flexible and, at first glance, held little emotional attachment. She stole an old Hermes scarf-tying guide from her mother, found at the bottom of her parent's bedside drawer when she was looking for spare change to score with. The yellowed-paper pamphlet was scented from the bottle of Miss Dior that rolled around the otherwise empty space and starkly chic with its plain-line drawings of chien French models with their scarves tied just so. This onion-thin sheet of paper taught her how to turn her scarf into a bag, turban, belt and even a jauntily soigné sling for a jetset arm broken on a ski slope but learning how to use it as an efficient tourniquet? That skill came from her older boyfriend who was experienced in teaching younger girls how to hit up for the first time.

Nowadays, her scarf still wasn't from Hermes but as she looped it around her neck, it made her imagine herself dodging the rain on a slick Parisian street instead of this small market town where the only

161

thing she tried to swerve around were memories. Instead of coffee bars with generic leather sofas where cappuccino was served after eleven a.m., there'd be a bar-tabac and a zinc counter for her elbows, heavily pitted with cigarette burns. It would smell of oudh, sebum and wormwood.

Her first scarf was scented with cheap patchouli from the local head shop which she mixed with a few drops of greasy oil from a bottle of musk and her Bonnie Bell skin cleanser. She fancied herself a perfumer after reading that truly stylish women made their own scents and thus smelled like nobody else on earth. These homemade touches mingled with the smell of the tan Iranian heroin that she cooked up in a tablespoon with its sweetly chemical smell like industrial BBQ sauce; the nostril searing zing of the citric acid used to break the drug down, and the salted-iron tang of the blood which she licked off her arm, after her hit.

When she had a room to live in, she had her own special drawer too, the place where she kept her kit; a little lacquered box for her drugs with a peacock on it, tail rayed out. That drawer developed its own smell, a damp plywood and chemical fug that peaked when the room warmed up and soon filled with bloodied discarded syringes.

Nobody told her that a smell or sound could trigger such powerful longings that she'd be flung back in time, carelessly unravelled back to the start point - her ground zero - the day she watched that film and read that book about Christiane and started to covet her poor, sad identity. Now, she has been straight for years, has remained straight for decades but sensory worm holes lie in wait, wriggling and reforming every time she thinks she has vanquished them. This response is visceral and then emotional and, lastly, rational. Her life is a landscape of strange longings and a seductive, crawling craving for those rituals and old

162

places where memories lie half buried and then become sedimented with layers of nostalgia and an idealised and romantic version of the ugly, grimy truth.

The Colours Of Snow

– Louise Tree –

The bull had leapt the hedge and the cow had taken him. She dropped her calf two days after Michaelmas, a winter calf. He would use up all his mother's milk - or so her father said. She could not help but think they might all share in it. But about this matter, her father seemed unusually determined, the silence settling upon him, whenever she began to speak of it.

Ruth went across to the cow house whenever she could. She loved the calves and they had never had a winter calf before. Father was always so careful. This one will grow to be a fine bull, she thought. Just like his father, Elijah. She had named their old bull when he was a calf – chose it from all the names in the Bible, running her fingers over the columns of stories in the fiery gloom of the parlour. Names formed a constellation in the dark, shone out to her from their deep eternity: Ezra, Saul, Abraham. Now, she sought a name for Elijah's son.

Two weeks later, her father had said, 'Ruth, take the calf into the side barn. He'll have no more of our milk. Go in each night and feed him the hay. Clean him out.' She was to care for him, until the spring came.

She was sad to take the calf from his mother, but they befriended one another as she shovelled the floor, spread the straw, replenished the hay. She was meticulous in her evening duty of feeding the little calf, of nurturing a new bull for the farm. She heard her mother say,

'For what good it will do him', beneath her breath. Ruth understood this to mean that hay was bad for calves – it led to the rot. Her mother said no more; and Ruth looked forward to the day when the spring grass would be fine and green. He will thrive then, she thought, when he joins the rest of his herd.

The old bull was strong, and inclined to wilfulness. His calf was gentle, his eyes expectant, unsuspicious, inclined even to playfulness. He had Elijah's colouring: creamy white half-curls sprawled along his back into patches of buff. He will be a beautiful bull, she thought. But as the weeks passed, and the trees were laid bare by scything winds, her vision of the young bull, growing sturdy in the lower field, became thinner, less tethered, began to shape itself into a wish. She could not decide on a name: she would choose one, conjure with it, then reject it as soon as she saw the little calf again. Nothing seemed to fit. Her father did not look her in the eye when she talked about the calf, rebuffed her suggestions for a name. Her mother would put her knitting down, rise from her chair and adjust the fire.

Now her mother stands at the farmhouse door. It is very cold, but she has left the door open. Her hands stroke her apron, slowly, unconsciously, as she watches her daughter, who stands between her and the barn. The wind pulls at Ruth's dress, tugs her hair from beneath her scarf. Her face is flushed with unspoken argument. Her mother can see the silent reasoning. *She is so clever*, her mother thinks, *for what good it will do*. She notices that her hair – so like her grandfather's – looks auburn under this mauve sky. She wants to smooth that hair down, stroke her daughter's head, lay it in her lap.

Ruth stares intently at the barn, its planks washed black and green by the winter rains. Her father reappears; he does not look at her, despite her entreaties, as he strides toward the sidebarn. He moves resolutely in his wiry, muscular way. In his face, the years of early rising, the mental calculations of stock and produce and the market, of negotiations with the factor, the money men. This calf, he reasons, is integral to all they have, is as vital as the stone which forms the walls of the house, is like the smoke that the chimney puffs into the kitchen, is the draught which runs through the house and makes his back ache. Ruth must learn this. No creature, no field, no season, exists alone. All things work together. Without this, they have nothing. She would always get so close to the animals – so impossible that she should feel so much. She must learn how to be a good farm manager. She must learn to be a farmer's wife. So she must grow up, and he must prove to her the ways of the world. God would approve the lesson. He is not doing this for the milk, or the rennet or the meat. It is all for her.

Yes, I know, she is thinking, *I know. You do not have to show me anymore. I do not flinch. I do my duty. I know my purpose.*

He is beside her now. She says, 'If the bull had not leapt the fence...'

'Enough.'

'I'll starve. I don't care. I don't care...,' her voice fades into a cry, as he passes her, and they both see her childishness. She follows him, her boots gathering mud as she runs along the edge of the field, as he turns into the sidebarn. The snow, which they had been expecting, begins to fall, in a swirl of large wet flakes. She shivers as she watches the calf, walking before her father on his long, new legs, toward the old, stone-floored shed.

She had seen so many young ones die, killed by some rule, some law, about the dairy, or the store cupboard, or the deal with the factor. They tell her it is the way; a necessity; God gave the animals to Adam, they tell her, for his use. They toil not, she argues, neither do they spin.

There is special providence in the fall of a sparrow. They don't believe her; and her words feel small.

Her mother watches from the darkening kitchen. *Let us both say no,* she thinks. *Let us save the calf. Let it grow.* A thought, so often kept down, seeps through. *We are the lost.* But she had never taught her daughter that. She had taught her deftness in curding, built her instincts in this, just as her mother had done for her. She had taught her the fine skills of sewing, and the finer skill of when to speak and be silent. Ruth must know the home is all things, as is the land. They are one and the same. They must fit the place given to them, just as birds explore a nesting place, check and check again their place of safety.

Suddenly, her daughter is so still she might be looking at the pillar of a temple, carved in the very form of girlhood, distilled, passive, like breathing stone. The wind has gone. The snow touches the girl lightly, hesitantly. *No,* her mother thinks, *the calf cannot be saved. Not this, or any other calf. Not this or any other daughter, no matter how fiercely we love. What good does it do?*

Ruth thinks, *In the Bible, God saved Isaac, he never meant him to be killed. It was a test. Surely now, this is all a test. I can change this story: I will be a better person, work harder, pray more and better.* She prays now, looking up into the blank, falling sky for an angel, with monumental white wings, swooping down with a staying cry. 'This, too,' he shows with his hand, 'is one of the Lord's children!'

Through the silence comes the deep, irregular reverberance of gunshot - a sudden, calculated charge; and the crows are spilt all over the field by the girl screaming, 'Let it live!' In the last turns and flutters of the birds, her voice vanishes. The damp snow flakes gain substance, thickening, drying. They begin to lay themselves down, quietly, like facts. They lay themselves upon the mud, upon every stone in the yard, and along the branches of the trees. Soon, they would fill all uncertain spaces.

The Friends

– Kathy Mansfield –

Max stabbed a final, satisfied full stop onto his report and sat back, surprised as ever at the speedy ending of an African day. He looked over the suddenly darkening garden, the scraping of the cicadas replacing the bird song, bats swooping like tiny Spitfires over the swimming pool and round the looming, purple Jacaranda tree in the corner. He jumped up, strode across the lawn, back to the house to get a Zambezi beer from the 'fridge, the first of the evening. He started to look forward to a Harare weekend: dinner at that new Chinese restaurant tonight perhaps, maybe a drive out to a game-park tomorrow. The phone rang before he reached the kitchen.

'Izzy? Hi! That's a surprise. Is everything okay?'

He'd had to call her in London only two days ago to check out some figures for his report. They were close friends, ever since their time together teaching in Botswana twenty years ago.

'Yes, everything's fine thanks. A quick call Max. You remember Sybil?' Izzy went straight to the point.

'Course I remember Sybil. I take your letters to her every time I pass through Gweru and put up with her little teas, don't I?'

'Anyway, listen, you know she's never been happy, stuck there in that little dump of a place.'

Sybil Viani, married to Giorgio, was a long-time friend of Izzy's. They had met in Botswana where Giorgio had worked for Rhodesia

Railways. When they'd all known each other Sybil had been a secretary to a Professor at the University. The growing capital on the edge of the Kalahari Desert had attracted more than its fair share of odd people in the early days of Independence, and Sybil had fitted in, in a spikey sort of way, with her English Literature quotations, her French poetry translations, her intimidating vocabulary. That she had an exotic, if slightly downmarket, Italian husband, added to her own eccentric persona: Giorgio, dark and slight, with thinning hair and a black moustache, speaking in the Italian ice-cream accent the English always find so comical.

He was hardly ever seen, especially during the tea parties Sybil held in their prefabricated bungalow near the railway station. Nobody knew much about him, except what Sybil told them when she was particularly upset with him – his drinking, and his rages. He had taken his shotgun to her one evening, nobody really knew why, and she had fled in her nightgown.

Max privately had some sympathy for Giorgio and could only put up with Sybil in small doses, and then only for Izzy's sake. She never stopped talking. Max couldn't understand Izzy's patience and carried messages and gifts between them only to please her.

And these days Sybil had no job and no people she could talk to, other than the other left-over Rhodesian whites in the railway apartment block on the edge of town; no allusions to French poetry in translation here. Even Max accepted she had been a woman of some interest, in her way, in Botswana, but now stranded in Gweru, she had diminished into an old lady.

Anyway, that had nothing to do with him. He dropped off Izzy's parcels from UK whenever he was on his way to Bulawayo, he put up with the teas, sometimes even a beer with old Giorgio.

In fact it was young Giorgio. Sybil was nineteen years older than him. Apparently that hadn't mattered all those years ago when they met in Zambia and he was mad for her, Italian and mad for her. But they never had children and as the years passed he drank more, went hunting with his friends on bush weekends and never learned to speak English properly. These fragments he had picked up over those dreaded tea times. Or, worse almost, he had jokey conversations with Giorgio, about Italian football or cars, while Sibyl fussed over the tea things and asked him what he was reading now dear? Max didn't suppose Giorgio had ever read a book in his life.

'Yes, I know she's unhappy. So what?'

'Well, she's left him at last. In fact she left him today and she'll be arriving at your place in about an hour or so, in a taxi.'

'What! Izzy, what do you mean, she's coming here? What do you mean?'

'Max stop shouting. Calm down. I told her in that letter you delivered last week, that you were staying in Harare a couple of weeks longer and if she really did want to leave Giorgio she should get on a National Motorways bus and come and stay with you. You can get her a ticket to London and I'll meet her at Heathrow. She's been talking about it for years.'

He couldn't speak, shock and outrage vying for first place in his response.

'I'll pay you for the ticket when you get back. Make her welcome tonight - you've got stacks of space in that guesthouse of yours. Just give her a chance to feel a bit better for a few days, and then...'

'That's not the point. I can't look after her. Can't she go to somebody else? There must be somebody else she knows here!'

'There is nobody else. She's alone, and she's old and she's doing a really scary thing. She has no money and she's coming back to UK after forty odd years in Africa. Come on Max.'

He took a deep breath and looked out of the hall into the garden. Only a couple of minutes had passed and his weekend was ruined. 'Why Izzy? Why do you have to be so involved and go to all this trouble?'

'There's no 'why' Max. She's my friend. If I was still there I'd manage it myself, but I'm not and you are.'

'Okay - okay. I'll see if I can get her a ticket for the Monday night flight. I can't stand more than the weekend.'

There was a moment's silence.

'Max, that's not all. I'm sorry, but it's not all there is to ask you.'

His outrage had subsided slightly as he had quickly calculated what would be involved and he could be rid of Sybil by Monday night. 'What? What else?'

'Please stay calm Max. She hasn't told Giorgio she's left him. She's scared to do that.'

'Just a minute, how do you know all this Izzy? What's going on?'

'She called me from the hotel phone at the half-way stop in Kwe Kwe two hours ago, and I've been waiting to make sure you're having your sun-downer before calling.'

'Well? So?'

'She's had to leave without any of her things. She's just got an overnight bag for a weekend visit. She told Giorgio I was in Harare and had invited her.'

'So? .... So?' Why did he repeat himself when he was agitated? He always did this. And what was she getting at?

'There's certain things she can't bear to leave behind. She was crying on the phone. I told her you would drive down and...' even Izzy paused here '...and tell Giorgio and collect her few bits.'

He couldn't speak. He couldn't believe what he was hearing. There was a long expensive silence between them. How long had he known Izzy?

'Izzy don't ask me to do this. I can't. I've no idea what to say, what to do. Christ Iz - he's an Italian!'

'Max…'

'No. I mean it. No!'

It had taken him three and a half hours to get to Gweru, longer than normal, driving south from Harare through a hot Saturday morning. He'd tried to concentrate on how much he always loved driving through any bit of Africa - golden, glimmering, endlessly stretching away in front of him. He'd left Sibyl, red eyed, frail, telling him to *do be careful dear*. He had her little list in the pocket of his shorts, it was bloody pathetic: some frocks, photographs, a brown leatherette manicure case - a gift from her brother in 1959. He didn't even know what leatherette was for Christ's sake.

Driving into Gweru he drove straight through the wide avenues to the plain apartment block set back on a small kopje of acacia trees, in yellow flower at this time of year. He had to get this over with. He parked in the bare earth car park at the back of the block, closed the car door firmly, and took some time to fiddle with the key, breathing deeply. He still didn't know what he would say to this man. How could he possibly tell him that his wife of 30 years wasn't coming back, had left him, and he, Max, was here to collect a few of her things? It was bloody impossible.

But he found words. He went in past Giorgio standing there unshaven in his vest and pants, and they said hello to each other.

'Ah, but Sybil is not 'ere today.'

179

'No. She's in Harare, at my place. She says she isn't coming back.'

He was really afraid as the little man exploded, striding up and down that box of a sitting room, and shouting for his shotgun, scrabbling through the sideboard drawer for his hunting knife, blaming Is-obel, blaming him. Max stayed quiet, white-faced. After the storm quietened both of the men stood stiff at opposite sides of the room, looking across at each other in a helpless silence. He suggested a drink and Giorgio came back from the kitchen with two icy cans of Castle beer, then slumped on the settee facing the tiny balcony. Max couldn't think of what to say, remained standing, glancing round and thinking that Sibyl might have been happier if she'd at least tried to make more of a home out of this place in five years - opened some of the cardboard boxes freighted up from Botswana stacked down the side of the room, half hidden by old table clothes, put up a picture, just tried a bit for God's sake.

The worst part was asking if he could collect the things on Sibyl's list. Of course he hadn't thought to bring anything to put the things in. Giorgio pushed a black dustbin bag at him, and then he had to force himself to go into the bleak bedroom, its two neat beds lying side by side separated by a small table. There was no window. He could hardly see what he was doing and was too stressed to look for a light switch. Giorgio started pacing again in the sitting room, cursing and blaming as he banged about. Part of Max's mind worried that Giorgio might rush in and knife him as he went through Sibyl's bedroom cupboard. How would that be explained to Max's family? How would Izzy explain that to them?

Oh God, why was he here? This was the worst thing he had ever done in his whole life. This wasn't how it was supposed to be, a stranger pulling together shreds from a marriage and stuffing them into a black dustbin bag, marking them off a wretched list.

- A yellow bloody cardigan.

- Three day dresses (what's a day dress for Christ's sake anyway?) and four pleated skirts, a particular pleated one in fawn (fawn – he thought that was a baby animal not a colour).

- That fucking leatherette manicure wallet.

- A faded photograph of a beautiful woman in a high necked Edwardian blouse, Sibyl's mother. He'd never thought of somebody as old as Sibyl as even having a mother.

Giorgio was standing with his back to the room, looking out over the balcony. He didn't look round as Max stood there and rustled the black plastic.

'It was zat abortion – it's always been the problem.'

Max swallowed. He couldn't say anything.

'These days nobodies cares if you're married or not. She couldn't get 'er divorce through. We didn't know what to do.'

Max fiddled carefully with the plastic bag, bending over it to fold the top, as if it was important, the way the folds were made and the exact type of knot he slowly wound it into.

It was over. He was driving back to Harare with the hot afternoon sun streaming through the passenger window. It had taken about an hour in Giorgio's place, but felt as if time had stretched so he'd lived more of his life than was possible. His stomach was cramped, and his heart felt sore. As he drove, he thought - about the hurt man behind him, the frail woman in front of him and the child she never had, of the life he had collected in the bag on the back seat, and how little there was of it. He thought of his own mum and dad, always together, always one. He thought about himself and his marriage and where he might be when he was old, and who would care about him. He couldn't believe he was crying, but he bloody was.

Charis

– Sharon Eckman –

Charis = 'favour' in the sense of favours given and favours repaid.
Also one of the three Graces.

Someone's here to see me and I almost know who he is. He's holding my hand all sticky. His nails are bitten down, fingers rough on my skin, and he strokes, gently, as though he's licking me.

"Fuck off," I say in out-loud words. In my head I'm saying: 'Thank you for licking me,' but I don't think he understands because his hand tightens and squeezes until I wonder if my fingers might pop with a balloon noise and he lets go, curling into his chair like a... what's that thing? Cheese trap standing on a chair... mouse. He's crying now and in my head I say sorry, but the coming-out words are "fuck off you stupid fuck-fuck."

I try to move my feet but they're sticky, there's a gunky sound when I lift them, a tired ripping that won't let me leave unless *They* say. Every time I try *They* put me back in my room, where it's too hot. The bed has lumps and the pillow smells of old, dark breath.

They say I chose the picture on the wall opposite my bed, the one in a garden with orange trees and a woman with a hat of flowers. There are three other women dancing with hardly any clothes on and a boy with wings shooting an arrow. I don't know why I'd have chosen it, because if you walk around here with no clothes on *They* throw a sheet

185

over you and carry you back to your room. I don't do that, but I've seen it happen to other people, the bald woman and the man who carries the doll.

I can hear noises - bells and clapping, drum beats and a whistle. And singing. They might be in my head, but when I turn to look, everyone else in the room is hitting or shaking things while one of *Them* dances with the woman who puts lipstick on her eyebrows. I know what *They're* really like though, when the licking man's gone. *They* don't dance. One of *Them* gives me a yellow thing to hold. She curls my hand around and makes me shake it so I can hear the rattle. I don't know what it's for so I throw it on the floor. She makes a tutting sound and I can hear she's pretending not to be cross because of the licking man.

Someone else is here and she's singing right at me. She has smiling eyes. She's shiny like an angel. I can smell her and it's different to the smells in here, the ones of piss cabbage mince that make me sick. And biscuits that don't even give you two dunks before they crumble into the tea so it's sludge tea. I remember how I like tea. Strong enough to stand a spoon up, no sugar. I've tried to tell *Them* but it all comes out wrong and *They* smile and nod when I say "Carpet tiling and no peanuts."

She's singing about a secret love. I know the words so I join in and they come out right, for once – and the man with licking fingers is crying, his nose flushed pink, his eyes are leaking I can't remember what but I don't like it. Have I done something wrong?

"Sheila, you remember the song!" he's saying and his voice sounds like sludge tea. And he's calling me Sheila, so that might be my name. The angel is still singing to me and her eyes are the colour of a knife.

She's wearing a blue dress with birds on it – small, bright, flashing, flying. I can't look away from them because they're moving, flying neatly, not hitting one another, dancing, flying and I reach out to touch them but the licking finger man pulls my hand back and the birds are quiet on the dress again.

"Fuck, fuck, poo, bastard," and this time I mean it, I don't mean to say: 'Thank you for licking me,' because the birds are quiet.

The angel says to me: "Do you want to touch?" I nod, because I don't want 'fuck poo' to come out of my mouth, instead of 'yes, yes let me touch the birds, let me fly into your dress and never come out.'

She takes my hand and her fingers aren't rough and licking, they are soft and warm like the top of a dog's head and I remember I had a dog. He was brown and soft, he was warm and licked away the leaking... the tears. The tears I had when... I don't remember that bit.

I touch the birds and my body rocks and floods with liquid. I can feel it move through and spinning, pooling in between my legs and shooting up and round and back and I make a sound I never thought I would again that wasn't in my mind. Out of my mind. The licking finger man jerks his hand away from me, his body mouse-curling small and he makes his own noise, a little wail of shock and shame. He's ashamed of me, because I'm feeling things and making sounds in this place, with its sheets and piss and looking in the mirror seeing a face that can't be mine. Fallen in and gaping mouth, skin gouged and lined, hair that droops and flops around as though it were tired of living on my head.

"I'm Charis," says the angel. "What's your name?" I struggle to look at her for a moment, still caught in the flood.

"Her name's Sheila," says the licking man when I don't answer. Is that really my name? I don't feel like a Sheila, but what would Sheila feel like? I don't want to be Sheila, I'm going to make one up.

187

"Fuck off," I say. "My name is Tinkerbell."

"Hello Tinkerbell," says Charis. Her voice has a laugh in it, but I don't mind. It's different to the way *They* laugh when I drop food out of my mouth because it tastes like poo and *They* push it back in.

"Don't forget our other residents! Sheila mustn't be greedy." One of *Them*, patting me on the hand. I can smell something sharp on her that hurts my throat. Charis has been kneeling in front of me but now her back straightens and she looks at the smelly woman. Her eyes are silver ice-fire cold and the smelly woman backs away with a huff, half scared half angry. I know all this. I don't know how, but I can feel *Their* feelings because Charis is here.

"I'll see you later," Charis bends towards me again and her smell is flowers and clean sky. She moves away and sings another song, but I don't know it and when she's gone *They* take me back to my room.

They've put railings up around the bed, because I keep trying to get out. *They* weren't mean this time when *They* put me in bed. *They* aren't always. There's one I like because she talks as though I'm still here and massages my hands and strokes my hair like I stroked my dog. She touches me as though I mean something.

It's too hot. Winter's outside because I've seen the trees without leaves. I remember winter and cold with... snow, soft like Charis's birds. I kick at the bedclothes to get away but they're too tight. The bedclothes and railings trap me in the heat and it's not a good burning, not like when Charis's birds were in me.

"It's all right, Tinkerbell, let me do it." And she's there, in the same bird dress, pulling the covers down so I can feel the cool air on my skin.

"Do they ever fly away?"

"Sometimes, but they always come back. They're messengers."

"What messages do they send?"

"They tell me where I need to be."

"Are you an angel? Or Holy-Mary-Mother-of-God?"

She laughs, high and cold. "Do you believe in angels, Tinkerbell? Or Mary?"

I think for a moment, lifting my fingers and letting them feel the air. "That's what I was told. Church on Sundays and Easter and Christmas, there was an angel on our tree. Its wings fell off one year because the glue was dry." And I thought God was dead and...

"I'm not an angel, or Mary. I've come to give you something, if you want it."

"Why me?" All my words are back, my mind works. I haven't had words for so long, I'm scared of them, they shock me like lightning. If this is a gift, I'm not sure I want it, because tomorrow I'll still be here with *Them* and the piss and poo and the knowing of it all. The song is in me and I know all the words now. "Did the birds tell you about me?"

"Yes, they tell me everything, and I tell them. See that painting on your wall? Primavera, the spring."

"Are you spring?"

"No. But I am Charis and I'm in there, and the gift is death, if you want it."

I stare into her silver knife eyes. People die here all the time and I've watched people fall away from me like ash from fire. I'm still here because I'm scared. Will it hurt, will I be alone, what's the last thing I'll see? And then what? I don't believe in God or Mary or heaven and hell, but I'm still afraid of where I might go. I had a cat that went away to die. Hoping to sleep and not wake up isn't the same as being told I can have it. I don't want the choice.

Charis is waiting patiently, watching me with those eyes that see inside, where I've hidden. She won't choose for me. "You won't get another chance," she says. I thought she was kind, but I'm not sure she is, and if she is, it's the kindness of a star, where you look up and think how perfect, but also how far away.

"The light from the stars you see, they're long dead. Do you want me to be kind?"

"What would it mean?"

"A soft gentle falling away. I can do that for you."

"Why me?" I ask again. There must be people more worthy – starving children, war refugees...

"Why not? You liked the song and saw the birds. And you have us on your wall."

I think about kindness and the falling away. And then I think about outside, not been or seen, tasted or felt for many measures of time. I'd like to be outside, although it's cold. I could be a dormouse or a hedgehog and curl up in leaves and something might eat me. I wouldn't mind. A fox, or a buzzard.

And then we're up and moving, Charis holding my hand and just before we pass through the door I look back expecting to see my body lying on the bed, like people say about dying, but it's empty; rumpled, impatient sheets tossed aside and I am still real, in a body that sags and crumples, points always downward. And nobody can see us, as we move through the corridors, under the constant, wearying lights.

I hear murmurs and muttering as we glide past open doors where others like me lie in their beds, curled into balls or clawing at the ceiling. In one room, *They* are trying to roll a man out of his leaking clothes but he's fighting *Them*. *They* aren't being mean, but *They're* stronger than he is.

We're out. I can see the stars and there's my favourite moon, the fingernail smiling moon and I smile back, even though the cold is creeping into me slow and steady, turning my blood pale blue like the edge of the sky.

Charis's hand is warm as she leads me past cars and gates, into the dark. When my cat went away, I searched streets and spider-filled sheds, knocked on unknown doors with a photograph but never found her. Perhaps I'll find her now.

"Choose anywhere you like, Tinkerbell." Charis's voice is the green of a spring leaf or birdsong at dawn. I look around but it's too dark for my eyes so I close them and feel with the part of me that touched the birds. Charis leads me on and we come to a tree with faces in the trunk.

"Can I stay here?" I ask and Charis lifts me and lays me down like a baby. She finds leaves to cover me and I giggle as she buries me in them, thinking of summers by the sea and my father reading his newspaper while we spaded him with sand.

I look up at Charis and she smiles with her kind-not-kind lips. "I think I'll go to sleep now," I say and she nods, so I close my eyes and wait for the spring to come.

Thin Walls

– Sarah Ridgard –

It was exactly half past seven when the first hammer blows of the day were struck in Victoria Road. They passed through the connective tissue between the terraced houses, the one-brick-thick party walls, vibrating along the joists and floorboards, making the bread crumbs jump on the kitchen counter at number 97, waking the starfish baby with a jolt in its moses basket at number 95.

Dean Havers had been awake since sunrise, dying to make a start on knocking down the back wall for the glass extension out into the garden. He'd bought the house for a steal in January, and wanted to get all the work done by September. *'Don't hang about, son. This bubble won't last forever.'* His father was in the trade, he should know, though he sounded more like a slaughterman when it came to taking on an old house. *'Get in quick and open it up,'* he said. *'Then gut it, clean up, and move onto the next one.'*

Dean picked out a sledgehammer. That should do the job. But first things first, he was just going to finish lowering the floor in the kitchen by smashing through the concrete with a pneumatic drill. The house wasn't going to know what had hit it.

The thuds from number 99 carried on down the hill, only becoming more muffled by the time they reached number 87 where Sylvie Godfrey lay awake in bed.

She clenched her fists at the noise. It annoyed her that someone was up early and getting on with their house renovations when her useless husband wasn't. And now next door were waking up as well. She could hear them laughing in bed through the wall. How she hated this boxy house, the way you could hear your neighbours breathing less than a foot away from your head at night; how she had to listen to their MFI headboard banging against the wall on Sunday mornings like it was desperate to end it all, while her husband lay next to her, either reading someone's thesis or fast asleep.

'See you in a week,' he'd whispered as he'd left for the airport earlier that morning. Sylvie checked her watch. He was going to a conference in Spain, and would be boarding soon.

This terrace was only ever intended as a first step on the ladder but for some reason Jonathan seemed more content to live in it these days as a home, rather than renovate it and move on up.

'We can't stay here forever.'

'Why not,' he'd say. 'I like it here,' and he'd look at the walls around them as if to say, *these do the job, don't they?*

That look at the walls, it infuriated her. Sylvie wanted to be up and away into a detached house with off-road parking and a pink Smeg fridge. And why stop there? She wanted another house, and then another one, maybe a second home in Cornwall and one in France.

It was all she could think about some days, her head in such a dizzy spin that she didn't know which of her three houses to live in next. The only problem was Jonathan. She hadn't factored in quite how useless he was at DIY. He might be an expert in microbial soil science but he didn't know an Allen key from a screwdriver, though he had make a couple of half hearted attempts on the house in the early days with a drill in one hand, an illustrated manual in the other, or *Idiot's Guide*, as

Sylvie liked to call it. Thank God for Niall then.

Sylvie murmured his name as she lay spread-eagled in bed. One of her husband's most promising and eager PhD students so far, Niall was coming round in an hour to lay the floating floor in the spare room.

By 9 o'clock, the whine of Black & Decker drills joined in with the general crash of building work as people donned dust masks and safety goggles, and got on with the job of improving their houses in Victoria Road. There were new kitchens to be taken out, newer ones to go back in, stud walls to bang up, others to knock down, till the houses didn't know whether they were coming or going.

Only the brace of black Labradors who got walked up and down the road every morning could hear how tired the houses were. The dogs cocked an ear at the timbers shifting and creaking as their joints were warmed through by the sunshine, at the draught which ran along the communal roof space like a long thin sigh.

For over a century, Victoria Road had withstood earth tremors and two world wars, even surviving the Baedeker raids in 1942 though the memory of the bombing was still held deep in their foundations, in the skirting boards that would never sit square on their tilting walls. Clifford Rodwell remembered that night all too clearly. He'd watched the city blaze from the terraced street where he'd lived his whole life.

'Catatonic Cliff' they called him either side. He never did anything, the neighbours said, except sit in front of the television or stare at a blank wall for hours on end. They thought his 'decline' must have started around the time his wife got carried off by cancer a year or two ago, though they couldn't be sure. Nobody could quite remember.

Sylvia's husband reckoned there was something of the holy man about him in his stillness.

197

'It's like he's meditating,' Jonathan said, not long after they'd moved into the row. But Sylvie just tutted. Here he was, an old man living on his own with that ghastly brick arch in the front room, and no doubt everything in his house was toxic and highly flammable.

'He could easily start a fire and then we'd all go up in flames. It would be safer for everyone if he went into a home.'

But more than the nylon carpets and the neglected front garden, what offended everyone the most and made them fear for their house values, was the acrow prop. It stood in the lounge beneath the arch, and had been there ever since the seventies when the son started knocking through the front room into the dining room in an attempt to create an 'open lounge'. He'd got as far as demolishing the partition wall, putting in most of the arch then lost interest in the job. So Cliff had put the prop in to make it safe and that put paid to any more home improvement projects. It might have taken a year or two but his wife did eventually get used to hoovering round it, and in those final months she'd even found it useful to grip onto when getting out of her armchair at the end of the evening.

There was a momentary lull in the midday sun. Dean removed his dust mask and Victoria Road drew breath. Babies took advantage of the quiet and napped in their cots; people stepped into their gardens and turned their faces to the sun. For the first time that day they noticed the birdsong from the cemetery, and how the scent of blossom from the Garden of Rest was being carried towards them on a gentle spring breeze.

'It's like living next to a green lung,' they liked to tell friends and prospective buyers, 'we're so lucky!' choosing not to notice the brown tip of the chimney just visible above the treeline, chuffing away in the winter months like a super-sized Lambert and Butler.

Sylvie was standing in the bedroom doorway, unable to take her eyes off Niall as he slotted the last of the laminate flooring together. He'd grown hot in the back bedroom and had already stripped off his tee-shirt.

'So, what do you think?' Niall squatted against the wall, his hands hanging between his thighs.

'Not bad,' Sylvie said, and tiptoed over the floating floor to put a hand flat to the wet heat of his chest.

It remained quiet some moments longer as if by rare agreement along the row. The light breeze died away and thoughts and dreams hung above the rooftops, not of heaven and the blue beyond, but of loft conversions and adding fourth bedrooms with Velux skylights and regulation stairs, of fortunes to be made and a mortgage-free life. Except above number 51 where dance halls and stockings were held together in a thick mesh of longing.

Cliff had finally reached 1947. For some weeks now, often with a hand to the cool steel of the acrow prop next to his chair, he'd been playing through the scenes in which he'd started courting Jean after the war, taking each one and slowing it down so that he could almost walk back into it and stand there in the flesh. It was April of that year, and after six months of seeing her wrapped in a thick coat through autumn and winter, he was just up to the evening when Jean, now in a dress and thin cardigan, was walking back with him from a dance where he'd been watching the ladder in her stockings creep higher and higher till it was well clear of her calf. He could make out every rung of those delicate nylon threads, till just the thought of putting one foot on the lowest rung and scrambling up to find out where those ladders might be headed made him so hot and bothered, he couldn't concentrate on half of what she was saying.

You're sweating fit to drop, Clifford,' she murmured, as she helped loosen his tie at the corner of her road, and eased the jacket from his shoulders.

By early afternoon, doorways and windows were belching out clouds of brick and plaster dust, and the contents of houses were being barrowed into yellow skips that stood in the road like open urns of bone rubble. The black dogs coughed and sneezed on their second walk of the day. They picked up their ears at the guttural moans from number 87 as Sylvie vibrated with Niall astride her husband's unused saw horse; flattened them at the scream of an angle grinder three doors along. Both dogs skidded to a halt at the gasp for breath that came from deep below ground like a death rattle.

Dean wasn't too sure what to do about the back wall. He'd knocked down half of it before getting distracted by another job which required the use of a sabre saw - one of his favourite power tools - in order to cut through some pipes in the kitchen. He was looking at the rear garden through the jagged hole in the brickwork, wondering if he should ring his dad who had more experience of these things, but then thought how much quicker he could get on if he finished bashing it down and then got himself over to the builders' merchant for a prop. He eyed up his tools and took a Kango breaker to the last of the wall.

The end when it came was swift, triggered by Dean's demolition of the load bearing wall, and helped on by his neighbours who had just finished digging out a cellar and undermined the foundations to their entire house; hastened by Sylvie's husband who'd cut a roof truss clean in half when he was trying to appease Sylvie after she'd gone on at him for a whole weekend about how useless he was and they'd never get a loft conversion done with him around the place. And so it happened. The weakened houses began to collapse down the hillside like a row of dominoes, a run that started at number 99 and reached the bottom in just seven and a half minutes, where it then turned the corner and flattened every house to the T junction and the cemetery gates.

Chimney stacks sheared off and toppled onto houses below, walls shunted into one another all the way along. Rafters sprung free of their roofs, spun through the air like cabers leaping four, five houses at a time before smashing through tiles and bedroom ceilings. Dreams went up in a mushroom cloud of brick dust that could be seen from the far side of the city, people turning their heads westwards at the groan of hundred-year old timbers being rent apart. Twisting vapours of pound signs evaporated into thin air along with broken beach apartments and pink Smeg fridges, everything smashed up and carried away in a cloud of smoke on a warm May breeze. Then silence.

It took quarter of an hour for the dust to settle before people could see that Victoria Road had been razed to the ground. All that remained was the yellow line of skips at the kerb, patiently waiting to be filled and taken away.

Yet out of the pile of smoking rubble, there emerged the outline of a single house. Somehow the run had leapt over that house, the roof from number 53 cartwheeling through the air to land on number 49 with such force that it blew the glass out of every window and blasted the front door clean off its hinges.

A crowd gathered at the front gate to number 51.

201

'It's a miracle,' someone said. 'There's not a hair on his head out of place.' A hush fell as the onlookers stared at Catatonic Cliff through the window sitting beneath his arch, the acrow prop by his side, wondering at this old man who remained so still like Buddha in contemplation while the houses met their end with a roar all around him.

Dean was weeping like a baby at number 99, buried beneath floorboards and a ton of roof slate, while six doors down the bodies of a couple lay pressed tight together, Niall pinioned to his floating floor by Sylvie on top, a slither of flesh compressed between slabs of brick and plaster like a hearty ham sandwich.

Meanwhile Clifford Rodwell, content and deaf as a post to the world, was in the late summer of 1947, his wedding night. He'd just found out for the first time where those ladders in his wife's stockings ended up, and was standing at the foot of their bed in a state of wonder.

A Canary In Kabul

– Antoinette Moses –

The bird had refused to sing for three days.

The owner was an Italian, who had fashioned a small restaurant in the Bagh e Bala district of Kabul. There were tables, red tablecloths, menus and an outside oven, built into the stone wall of the building. The girl had never seen any customers, though she imagined that there were foreigners who came there in the evenings to eat pizzas and listen to the owner's scratched recordings of Verdi operas.

The canary, named Giovanni after the patron saint of the Italian's home city of Florence, did not appear to be in good health. It was moulting. The floor of his small bamboo cage was littered with small pillows of feathers as if the canary had decided to furnish himself with comfortable seating areas.

'I offer him mango – he loves mango – pasta, rice. He's not interested. What can I do?' asked the Italian.

'Maybe he's having a rest,' the girl ventured. She knew nothing about canaries.

The girl had met the Italian by chance. It was the summer of 1971, and she was in Kabul with her boyfriend, Nick. Kabul because Afghanistan was one of the places one went to in 1971. Journalists called it the hippie trail, but the words seemed wrong. A trail should lead somewhere. She thought it was more like the Grand Tour; there were obligatory ports of call. The difference between the two itineraries was that the hippie trail headed east and ignored the cultural artefacts of the countries along the way, whereas the earlier travellers visited Europe and bought as many artefacts as possible. All the foreigners she'd met in Afghanistan and Nepal wanted to acquire what they felt was Eastern spirituality as if it was something that you could get through osmosis. Or drugs. Or both. They visited Kabul and Goa and Kathmandu, and some travelled to Kashmir where you could live on a house boat on Dal Lake. The girl had wanted to go to Kashmir. She imagined herself and Nick under an awning of painted silk. They would drink tea and she would read him her poems and he would talk to her.

Nick wanted to go to Kabul because he wanted to go to Mazir-i-Sharif where it was said you could buy the best hash in the world. She wanted whatever he wanted. They had been together for four months and she had thought that the trip would bring them closer together. She had thought it would be splendid, but it felt more like an extended holiday without comfortable hotels. But she smoked the hash that was better than that she'd found in London, and the days blurred.

The Italian was old, she thought, at least fifty. He wore a jacket and a tie and the buttons of his jacket were done up even though the day was hot. They had met in Chicken Street where she was shopping for food.

A few days after they had arrived in Kabul, Nick had discovered that an informal hotel for hippies was being run in a large, once elegant, house in the Shahr-e-Nau district which offered free accommodation for a cook. The girl had no training or experience as a cook apart from making meals for friends and family, but was happy to allow Nick to boast of her skills. In reality, the lack of produce meant that as long as food was produced twice a day, nobody minded what it was. On the first day she went to the meat market where, if you clapped your hands, the flies rose up and the black meat was revealed to be red. The hotel would be vegetarian, she decided.

She made onion and potato soup, onion and potato curry, and potatoes with onions and tomatoes. She added aubergines and peppers, when she could find them, and lentils and rice. For protein they ate almonds. For sweetness she threw raisins into the rice and they ate mangoes. The day she met the Italian she was buying eggs to make a potato and onion omelette since the eggs she'd previously bought had proved to be foul, filling the kitchen with sulphurous fumes.

When the Italian met her, he was buying flour which had American aid stamps on the bags, and she was trying to communicate with the stall-holder. She spoke no Farsi, the stall-holder spoke no English. Moreover, she had no idea how to test eggs, though she did have some distant memory that buckets of water were involved. Not that there was either a bucket or water at hand.

The Italian watched her lame mime of cracking open a bad egg and smelling it and came to her rescue. He picked up an egg, shook it gently and gave it to the girl. She shook it, nothing happened.

'E buono,' he said. 'Good.'

'Khoob,' said the stallholder. The Italian picked up another one and handed it to her. She tentatively shook it. It rattled as if it contained ball bearings.

'That one's no good,' she said in Italian.

She had spent a year in the country and spoke the language fluently. And while she did not know much about eggs, beyond how to cook them, she was fairly certain that they should not rattle. She smiled. She was now empowered to distinguish eggs that might be edible from those that clearly were not.

'Bad,' she said in English to the stall-holder.

'Bad,' replied the stall-holder.

The girl thanked the Italian and bought two dozen eggs, shaking each one gently as she tested them for their inner dislocation. It occurred to her that for an egg to rattle it might be further along the road to being inedible than those at home which had merely gone a bit stale. The notion of best-by dates had not yet been introduced in English supermarkets.

Having discovered that she spoke his language, the Italian insisted that she visit his restaurant. The girl could not go there immediately since she wanted to get back and cook the eggs before they began to rattle. It was days since she had eaten an egg.

The following day she walked to the Italian's restaurant. He gave her a glass of his acidic, dark pink wine and introduced her to Giovanni.

'Listen to how he sings,' said the Italian.

The girl came from London and knew only the squawks and purrs of sparrows and pigeons. The canary trilled and chirped as it perched on its twig clearly aware of his audience. There was a great variety of sounds, she thought, as if the small bird was echoing a hillside of birds.

'What a Caruso,' said the Italian.

'He's marvellous,' she agreed, having never heard a canary. 'Exceptional.' The following year, in Greece, she found that the owners of the kebab shops put their caged canaries near the kebab rotisserie to make them sing louder. They were also proud of their birds.

'Where I grew up there were always canaries,' said the Italian. He told her he came from Florence and was overjoyed to learn that she knew his city. He had not been back, he said, for twenty-five years.

'All my life,' said the girl. It occurred to her that he must have left Italy at the end of the War.

'I can't go back,' he said.

The girl wondered why, but felt it would be rude to ask. Her mother had frequently told her that she asked too many questions like the elephant's child. She had been given the Kipling story to read as a warning. Why remained her favourite question.

'Why do you think he can't go back?' she asked Nick, but he did not hear her, or was uninterested, since he did not reply.

The following week the Italian told her about the Paghman water which they used for drinking. It was the sweetest water she had ever tasted. There were beautiful gardens in Paghman, like the Tivoli gardens in Rome, he said. It was cooler there.

The girl thought that the name sounded magical, like the hanging gardens of Babylon and decided not to visit them. They were bound to disappoint, although Kabul, itself, did not disappoint her. She loved the closeness of the mountains, the clarity of the air. The way you could walk in the streets and markets unmolested. She planned to visit Bamiyan which had lakes the colour of the local lapis lazuli.

She visited the Italian every day. He taught her how to cook a Florentine dish called *gnudi* which was a kind of miniature dumpling with cheese and spinach, and played her Tito Schipa singing "*E lucevan le stelle*".

'It's from *Tosca*,' he said. 'Cavaradossi is about to die. He remembers his love. The stars were shining and he has never loved life more. Or wanted to die less.'

'Tosca's my mother's favourite opera,' she told him, but thought this was strange even as she said it, since her mother rarely showed emotion and disliked poetry. 'It must be wonderful to love like that,' she added.

And it must be wonderful to feel that acutely about life, she thought. If she shut her eyes she could smell the sage and oil and hear the music. It would be like being back in Italy. Was she happier there? Should she go back?

'Just imagine,' she said, 'we are sitting in a café in Florence. And I'm writing poems in a little book with marbled papers which I've just bought in a little shop near the palazzo Corsini.'

'I know the shop,' he said. 'They bind books. Is it still there?'

'It was still there two years ago,' she said. 'It was near my hotel.'

'I worked in a hotel not far from there. In the Piazza di Santa Maria Novella. The Grand Hotel Minerva.'

Oh,' she said. 'I never dared go in there. I was in a tiny place. The room was so small that the door wouldn't open fully even with a single bed.'

'Everybody came to the Minerva. We had Greta Garbo, Schipa himself, Hemingway, Hitler.'

She was remembering her cheap hotel. It was near the station, not the river, she recalled. 'And the hotel had fleas,' she said.

He looked at her legs then which were spattered with a rage of bites. She saw him look.

'It's the chairs in the house,' she said. 'They're full of fleas. And lice. I go to the Intercontinental Hotel every morning and swim and use their shower, but I can't get rid of them.'

'I have something,' he told her. He went into the kitchen and came out with a paper bag filled with a greyish powder.

'Use this,' he said. You can put it on the chairs, too.'

She dusted herself with it later that evening and a confetti of dead insects fell out of her hair. The same happened to the chairs. The powder killed everything. She went to thank him.

'What is it?' she asked him.

'DDT,' he told her.

'It works brilliantly,' she said. Another English girl at the house had lent her some calamine lotion and she was now painted pink, but the itching had abated. That was also the day that Giovanni began to sicken. She told the guests about the canary over supper.

'Perhaps Giovanni needs company,' said Lucy, an American artist who was on her way to India to find an ashram.

The girl looked at Nick who was talking with Joseph, a recent arrival at the house. Nick spent all his time now with Joseph, talking together until the early morning or when she fell asleep. She disliked Joseph, not because he was unlikeable, but because he needed Nick's company. She would win, she knew, because she and Nick would move on together. But she was not sure what kind of triumph this would be.

'Why do you think he mentioned Hitler?' she asked Joseph. They were discussing the Italian again. 'Do you think he was a war criminal?'

'He's just a man,' said Joseph. 'He got stuck in a place.'

About a year later she would see Joseph's name in an article in the Sunday Times. He had become a heroin addict and died in Kabul. The writer lamented a wasted life and wondered who this young man was. She felt she ought to write to him and tell him about Joseph. How his brother had died, the gifted, brilliant brother who was everything that Joseph couldn't be. How Joseph believed he was expected to fill his brother's shoes and knew he couldn't. How he'd bought a multi-coloured coat in the market, and they'd laughed because of his name, and because she mixed up Jacob and Joseph.

Joseph was a man who got stuck in a place.

She never wrote to the journalist.

Years later, when she thought about Kabul, when it was razed to the ground, when there was no longer a garden in Paghman, it was always the Italian she remembered. She was not sure why. Was it the small core of Italy he had contrived within the alien city, she asked herself. Or was it the canary?

You're In The Movies, Huni

– Isabelle King –

Falling for the director of a low budget sci-fi film could be precisely the reality check you need in order to stop making bacon toasties and progress with your life.

Your progression begins like this. You are a twenty-seven year old woman crawling on your hands and knees across the kitchen floor. You are playing a futuristic two-headed space monster. You open your mouth as wide as the prosthetics will permit and imitate an enormous silent scream. The vocal scream, the production assistant informs you, will be added in a post-production ADR session. You are strangely looking forward to screaming in the ADR session because it's the only sound you make in a film in which you don't have any lines. As the only person in the film, there is nothing to actually say. The film is set during a time when monsters have invaded earth. A normal girl comes home from her normal job and finds that her normal kitchen is occupied by a not-so-normal two-headed space monster. The girl looks terrified; the two-headed space monster screams threateningly at her, the film ends.

Ok, it's not a great story but this short film is supposed to be a pilot for a feature, mainly a showcase for the film crew's VFX skills. The team don't have the budget to cast two actors so they cast you as both the normal girl and the not-so-normal intruder.

You wear bright red prosthetic make up with fake teeth. The prosthetics squash your nose, exaggerate your forehead and furrow your eyebrows into a fierce frown. Your hair is scraped back, there are black contacts in your eyes and your fake teeth protrude eccentrically from your mouth. Your stomach muscles ache from crawling and the fake teeth taste like that plastic toy 'phone you used to chew as a kid. You are aware you look grotesque but this doesn't bother you. This is not the most unusual thing you have ever done. There was that one time you played a talking house with chicken feet in a kids' show about fairy tales. That time you played a ballet-dancing broken wind-up doll. That time you played a creepy tree.

As for being two-headed, the editor tells you that she will add the second head in post production, a duplicate of your current one. You are not that talented an actress that you can develop another head.

This film is £100 a day which is the most you've been paid for a short; accommodation and food is provided. The film set is well organised and the crew are the correct amount of 'stressed but in a friendly way' that you could hope for. It comes as a welcome change from the hardware store where you work 'in-between jobs'. Your days are filled with selling DIY tools about which you know nothing and telling people that the *doobries* come with batteries included. In the highly probable instance that you are wrong about this however, you cover yourself by casually mentioning the store's flexible refund policy. You live in a tiny flat in East London with two other actors. The walls, you are convinced, are made from cardboard. You hear all the conversations of the neighbouring couple who frequently argue about who is the most selfish and who drank all the wine. The shower in your flat is a converted closet above the staircase; it leaks onto the stairs below and it's only a matter of time before it collapses. You eat cheap pasta pots and processed sausage rolls from supermarket 'reduced' sections. You cry down the phone to friends: "I haven't had acting work for months!"

"You did that Crisps advert remember? That aired last week. *Now in old un-washed sock flavour!*"

This life-style has gone on for years. You are aware that it's out of hand but it's the only way you know. Sometimes a theatre tour in the UK or abroad. Sometimes a short film. Sometimes voicing talking zebras, bats and porcupines for cartoons. Sometimes nothing. Sometimes hardware stores. But this is what you signed up for. You spend your days doing dull jobs and your evenings practising for auditions. You wait for 'the call'.

Often, you're practising for so many different auditions at once you get confused and go all Chekov at a village panto casting . You're thinking 'Uncle Vanya' even though that's tomorrow, you're ahead of yourself, you say your lines with grave sincerity, "Don't worry Cinders, for I, Buttons, shall take you to the ball." You will not get 'the call'.

And then there are times that you fall for the directors of low budget sci-fi films, a matter which requires the grave sincerity of Chekov and you should be getting your 'Uncle Vanya' on right now, but you get confused again and end up back in panto land.

Enter Daniel. Stage right. Looking villainous. Audience boo.

Daniel has the sort of look that makes women start talking uncontrollably about how good they are at multi-tasking and face painting and cake baking and cute stuff. You are an intelligent, fully grown, kick-ass woman who suddenly feels the need to demonstrate how nurturing and soft and silly round the edges she can be. You can't seem to help it.

Daniel has the kind of face that makes you want to tuck his hair behind his ear, even though his hair is short and you will tuck nothing but thin air. Daniel has the kind of stance that makes you want to tilt your head and stare, just stare, the kind of mouth that makes you want to edge forward slowly. 'Lean on me' is the catchphrase written on his forehead.

You know that falling for Daniel is a bad idea. You know this to be true and still you stare at him dotingly from across the table in the pub. It's a Friday evening, one week after filming, and he has driven out to see you at your local in East London. You are suddenly aware of how big and googly your eyes are. This situation requires 'evening eyes' but your eyes need to be like Daniel's - small, dark and narrowed with lustful intent. You squint your big, googly eyes.

"You were terrific," Daniel tells you. "That was a tough gig I gave you but you nailed it, every damn shot."

"Thanks, I do my best."

"You back at the hardware store now?"

"I've moved on."

"To a better place?"

"To a fry up cafe. I make a mean bacon toastie."

Laugh, laugh, laugh. It's all very playful. You smile at each other over your glasses of wine, him with his gorgeous eyes, you with your squinty evening eyes.

"From futuristic two-headed space monster to bacon-toastie maker, your talents know no bounds."

Daniel has driven out to see you for a reason. He knows what it was. You know what it is.

Outside, he flings you up against his car parked on the road opposite the pub. You kiss. You have him. He is in your arms. He presses himself firmly against you. You feel it hard through his jeans. It's no longer playful. It's earnest.

"Lean on me."

218

You lean. You lean. You lean.

Then he is gone. Needs to drive home. You don't know what you were expecting from the evening but it's too late to go back. You are all emotions now. You can't wait for Daniel to call and chat about what happened and where you will go from here. Your Daniel.

Except he isn't your Daniel. He is Elena's Daniel. Elena is his girlfriend. They have been going steady for over a year. Elena is a First Class Honours BA Textiles graduate and designer of quirky dresses for fun-loving women. Elena is shabby chic. Elena eats sweet potatoes instead of chips. But occasionally Elena will steal the last chip from your plate and you will find it audacious and adorable. Elena would not be seen dead portraying a futuristic two-headed space monster in a low budget sci-fi film. Elena doesn't do 'grotesque'. Elena would never make the mistake of kissing a guy up against his car until she has first secured him as her official boyfriend. You know this about Elena the second you see her picture on Facebook. Elena takes a good selfie, both eyes in strong focus.

You skip breakfast. You don't sleep. You sit around in wet towels for hours after taking a shower. You stare at the walls. You go for long walks. You come home. You go out again. You wish you would melt. You compose text messages only to delete them.

Oh hey Daniel, I hope your bowels feel relieved after you took that massive shit on my heart.

Oh hey Daniel, interesting that I should be in your futuristic film seeing as your views about women are from the past.

Oh hey Daniel, fuck you Daniel.

Daniel, how's your girlfriend? How's Elena? You...you...

Daniel, I'm in love with you. Please kill me. Do it quickly. Thank you and goodnight.

You settle on texting him: *Hey you, fancy a chat?*

When your phone starts buzzing you let it ring several times before you pick up.

"Hey."

"Hey, how you doing?"

His voice comes with batteries included and is non-refundable. He sounds so normal, upbeat, chilled. You begin to doubt yourself. Was your intimate moment as passionate as you remember? Did he bite your lip hard several times or was it more of a cheeky nibble?

"Oh, good thanks! Great. Yeah I'm cool," you say, trying to sound chirpy. "I um....I wanted to chat about last Friday."

"Oh yeah, what about it?"

Did you really feel his penis or was it just a very stiff bit of jean?

"Well, you know, what happened?"

"Oh yeah, what happened?"

You start to cry. You hate yourself for crying and the more you hate yourself the more you cry.

"I...I thought you'd remember."

"Oh, oh that, yeah, yeah, yeah that, no that was just a bit of fun."

But you were so sure it was earnest. There were feelings involved. You felt them.

"Well, what about Elena?"

He will surely buckle at this. But Daniel doesn't do buckling. Daniel is one cool cowboy.

"Oh," he says casually, "she's fine, she knows how it goes. You know, when people make films together, stuff happens. That's it, that's just film biz, you know."

That's film biz.

"You never told me you had a girlfriend."

220

"You never asked."

You say nothing. There is nothing to say.

"Why?" he asks. "What did you expect?"

What did you expect? You don't know. When you're working in a hardware store one day and playing a futuristic two-headed space monster the next, it's hard to know what to expect from anything. You spend your life hopping madly from one temporary job to another, from one bonkers endeavour to the next, no grounding, no security, no sense of direction, everything up in the air, yourself included. You are all air. No one will ever take you seriously when your life is ridiculous. No wonder Elena isn't bothered. She can't lose her boyfriend to a bit of film biz, a bit of fun, a bit of air.

You make bacon toasties and question your life choices. You realise that what happened with Daniel reflects everything that's wrong with your life. People can treat you however they want when your life revolves around realising their vision and never having the time to realise your own. You are going to stop reading from other people's scripts and write your own script.

The film crew don't call you back for an ADR session. When the film gets its online release you watch it for the first time at home, in your pyjamas, dipping crackers into houmous. You see yourself as a normal girl with a normal job coming home to her normal kitchen. You see yourself as a futuristic two-headed space monster. You dip your crackers into the houmous. It is unusual to see yourself as a normal girl. A futuristic two-headed space monster feels like the norm. This highlights every shade of what's stupid about your existence.

You see yourself scream at the end of the film. The film crew have used another woman's scream in post production. You see your mouth in all its fake toothed eccentricity move but another woman's scream

221

comes out. You feel cheated.

Your friends start to phone.

"Woooaaa, great film, you were amazing!"

"They used another woman's scream," you tell them.

"Does that matter?"

"Yes, it does."

This is the start. The start of your script. There will be no stolen screams from low budget sci-fi films, no chicken feet, no talking zebras, no new flavours of crisps, absolutely no Daniels. There will only be you. It's not going to be easy. There is so much work you have to do. But it will be worth it. In years down the line people will ask how you came to be the person you are today and you will tell them that, sometimes, you have to take a good hard look at yourself.

Contributors

Ann Abineri trained as a nurse, brought up four children, studied with the OU and now teaches in the childcare and education sector. Although frequently tempted by writing courses, Ann now puts time aside to follow her own writing interests and has had success in the last year with poetry, flash fiction and short stories.

Deborah Arnander has a PhD in French literature, and works as a literary translator. She won an Arts Council Escalator award in 2010, when she began her first novel, *The Cinderella Watch*, which was shortlisted in 2014's TLC Pen Factor competition. She has published stories in *Unthology One* and *Words and Women One*, both with Unthank Books, and has poetry in the webzine Ink, Sweat and Tears, and in various anthologies published by Gatehouse Press. She lives in Norwich.

Lynne Bryan is the author of a short story collection, *Envy At The Cheese Handout* (published by Faber & Faber), and the novels *Gorgeous* and *Like Rabbits* (Sceptre). Her work has been included in many anthologies and has been broadcast on the radio and adapted for film. She is co-organiser of Words And Women.

Susan K Burton spent 14 years in Japan, lecturing as an associate professor in Japanese universities. She has co-authored two academic books, and written for the Telegraph, Times Higher Education, and Going Down Swinging. Now based in Norwich, she is studying for a PhD in Creative and Critical Writing at the UEA where she is investigating the unusual lives and bizarre livelihoods of foreigners in Japan.

Caroline Davison is a historian, writer and musician from Norfolk. Her novel *The Pleasure Garden* was published in 2006 by Piatkus. Her children's book *The By-Mistake Guide to Norfolk* was published in 2012. Caroline has worked as a teacher of English as a Foreign Language, a conservation officer, and a freelance historic environment consultant. She is currently Director of the Norfolk Archaeological Trust.

Sharon Eckman was Time Out Travel Writer of the Year in 1995 and her non-fiction has appeared in broadsheets and travel magazines on topics ranging from hunting in Namibia to science fiction fans in London. She was longlisted for the Fish Memoir Prize 2015 and shortlisted for the Words And Women 'About' competition in 2014. Her first novel is currently out with agents and her short story, *Dinner for Four*, will be published in Shooter Lit's 'Surreal' edition in January 2016.

Sarah Evans has had over a hundred stories published in anthologies, magazines and online, with outlets including: the Bridport Prize, Unthank Books, Lighthouse, Structo and Best New Writing. She has won a number of short story prizes, including the Winston Fletcher Prize, the Stratford Literary Festival Prize, the Glass Woman Prize, the Fylde Writers' Circle Prize and the Rubery Prize. She has also had work performed in London, Hong Kong and New York.

Belona Greenwood is a former journalist who escaped to Norwich where she did an MA in Scriptwriting at the University of East Anglia. She has won an Escalator award for creative non-fiction, is a winner of the Decibel Penguin prize for life-writing and writes plays for adults and children. She is a Director of Chalk Circle Theatre Company, and founder and co-organiser of Words And Women.

Victoria Hattersley lives in Norwich, works in publishing and has a six year-old daughter. She began writing in 2013 and has had stories published in *Unthology 6* by Unthank Books (Norwich) and *Before Passing* by Great Weather for MEDIA (New York). In addition to writing short stories, she is currently working on her first novel, *The Lantern Man*.

Emma Healey grew up in London where she completed her first degree in bookbinding and was the third generation of women in her family to go to art college. She then worked for two libraries, two bookshops, two art galleries and two universities, and was busily pursuing a career in the art world before writing overtook everything. In 2008, after the death of one grandmother and the decline of the other, she began to explore the idea of dementia in fiction, and she moved to Norwich in 2010 to study for the MA in Creative Writing at UEA. Her debut novel, *Elizabeth is Missing*, was published to critical acclaim in 2014, became a Sunday Times bestseller and won the Costa First Novel Award.

Danusia Iwaszko is a playwright who lives in Bury St Edmunds, and works regularly in the region and throughout the country. She is Artistic Associate at The Theatre Royal Bury St. Edmunds, for whom she wrote the musical *A Labour of Love* in 2015. Her plays have been produced by Eastern Angles, Theatre Royal York, Studio 503, Menagerie Cambridge and she was attached writer at The National Theatre Studio in 2006. She regularly leads writing workshops and runs her own theatre company The Hal Company.

Sara Keene (@SaraKeene) has spent most of her career in show-business PR, first as a film publicist and latterly as the press representative for a number of actors and directors. She recently completed the Creative Writing MA at Birkbeck College and is writing a novel inspired by her experience of life at the heels of the famous. She claims it will be entirely fictional. She is also planning a children's book about a boy and his very unusual dog.

Julie Kemmy has been writing for pleasure since she was about 12 years old, and in more recent years has been writing character studies, short stories, and the outlines of bigger ideas. She works full-time so usually it is only on holidays that she achieves anything. She would describe herself as a great reader and admirer of other good writers, with a lot to learn.

Isabelle King is an actress, writer and producer. She's the founder of Books Talk Back; literary events which support and showcase new writing talent. Isabelle's writing has been short-listed for the Ideas/Writers' Centre Norwich national fiction competition and she won an arts journalism competition to be the Embedded Writer at the Family Arts Conference 2015. Isabelle has written a children's book of short stories and frequently reads them at family events throughout Norfolk.

Kathy Mansfield was runner up in a competition by Leaf Books in

2006 with *The Steady Bookkeeper* which was published as a single short story, set in Malawi. She does not write about stereotypical 'African' tragedies: famine, war, destitution. She writes about the other Africa: a complex, energetic and optimistic continent of fifty four very different countries. Her current project is a collection of short stories set in the context of Zimbabwe and its sometimes violent efforts to change from a white-owned system of agriculture to one which reflects the larger population.

C.G. Menon has won a number of short story awards, including the Asian Writer prize, the Winchester Festival award and The Short Story prize. Her stories have been broadcast on radio and are published or forthcoming in journals including The Lonely Crowd and anthologies such as Siren Press' *Fugue II*, the Rubery Book Award short story collection, the Willesden Herald shortlist and the first Words And Women collection. She lives in Cambridge, and is currently working on her first novel.

Margaret Meyer is a writer, therapeutic counsellor and bibliotherapist. She has worked in schools, museums, and is currently a reader-in-residence in the prison service. Before training in psychology she was a fiction editor with Hodder & Stoughton NZ, publisher for the Museum of London, and director of literature for the British Council, promoting UK writers around the world. A former journalist, Margaret's non-fiction has been widely published. Her latest, an essay on 'not knowing', is included in the forthcoming *The Wisdom of Not Knowing*, published by Triarchy Press.

Nicola Miller is a columnist and features writer for a paid-for weekly newspaper called The Bury Free Press and is based in West Suffolk. She usually writes about landscape, books, and food. She has her own website, *The Millers Tale*.

Antoinette Moses is a graduate of the UEA Creative Writing MA and also completed a creative/critical PhD on documentary theatre. Prior to becoming a full-time writer, she had a long career in arts administration and journalism. She re-founded and directed the Cambridge Animation Festival, worked for the Norfolk and Norwich Festival, and edited Direct, the journal of the Directors Guild of Great Britain. She has written a number of plays which have been produced in Norwich and Cambridge, and also published over twenty books of language-learner literature, three of which won the Extensive Reading Award. She lives in Norwich and teaches creative writing at UEA where she also produces FLY, the Festival of Literature for Young people.

Patricia Mullin was shortlisted for an Arts Council East Escalator Award in 2009. Her 2005 novel *Gene Genie* was republished as an e–book in 2012. Two short stories, *The Sitting* and *The Siren,* were published in *Words And Women: One* 2014 and *Words And Women: Two* 2015 respectively. Her novel *Casting Shadows* was commended in the Yeovil International Literary prize 2014, judged by Elisabeth Buchan. In 2015 Patricia was awarded an Arts Council England grant to re-draft *Casting Shadows*.

Glenys Newton is a mum, storyteller and writer - in that order. Up until a few years ago, Glenys worked as a social worker and gave it all up to study storytelling. She packed her job in, sold the house and lived in an old post office van for a year, and went around telling stories to whoever would listen. Glenys won the internationally acclaimed Moth True Stories Told Live in 2014 and appeared on Radio 4 in 2015 to talk about storytelling. More recently, Glenys has become involved in volunteering with refugees as the ever increasing humanitarian crisis spreads through the lands. Glenys will be touring with a performance of refugee stories throughout 2016.

Dani Redd is in her second year of a PhD in creative and critical writing at the University of East Anglia. She has recently completed a draft of her first novel, *Vore*, a darkly comic dystopia, and is currently halfway through a second, *Bodeg*, which is set on a fictional island in the Arctic Circle.

Sarah Ridgard is a graduate of the University of East Anglia with an MA in Creative Writing. She won a place on the Escalator Literature programme run by the Writers Centre Norwich in 2009, and three years later went on to publish her debut novel, *Seldom Seen*, with Random House. The novel was longlisted for the Desmond Elliott Prize 2013 for new fiction, the New Angle Prize for Literature and shortlisted for the Authors' Club Best First Novel Award. Sarah lives in Norwich and is currently working on her second novel.

Claudine Toutoungi trained as an actress at LAMDA and has worked as a BBC radio drama producer and teacher. In 2014 her play *Slipping* premiered at The Stephen Joseph Theatre, Scarborough. Her radio adaptation, starring Andrew Scott and Charlotte Riley, was nominated for three awards at the 2015 BBC Audio Drama Awards. Other theatre and radio credits include: *Deliverers* (BBC R4), *Home Front* (BBC R4), *Bit Part* (Stephen Joseph Theatre Scarborough), *Outside In* (Junction,

231

Cambridge) and *Life Skills* (Shared Experience at the Hampstead Theatre). She was a UK Arvon/Jerwood Foundation mentee, working with Colin Teevan. Her poetry features in the 2015 anthology *New Poetries VI*, (Carcanet), has appeared in a wide range of publications and in 2015 was shortlisted for The Bridport Prize.

Louise Tree is a writer and scholar. Her work explores the ways in which we imagine the past and how stories can speak to one another. Her literary passions are fairy tales, Shakespeare and Virginia Woolf. Current writing projects include a monograph on history writing in the reign of Anne, and a novel about war and memory. She has a PhD in History of Ideas and has interests in women's writing and the writing of history in the eighteenth century. She teaches History as an Associate Lecturer at Anglia Ruskin University and has taught English Literature, Philosophy and History for many years.

Lightning Source UK Ltd.
Milton Keynes UK
UKOW02f1943240316

270817UK00002B/29/P